KING

————

(LONDON BOYS I)

REBECCA CASTLE

ISBN: 9780645395976

To my friends in London.
Thank you all for the best ten years.
Cheerio.

"Next to being married, a girl likes to be crossed in love a little now and then."

PRIDE AND PREJUDICE

I'm not able to.

I'm rooted to the spot. My mind is a total mess.

We're surrounded by people here – surrounded by the best security in the whole of Britain guarding the Crown Jewels - but right now it's like no one else even exists and it's just him and me in our own world and I can't even *freaking* move.

I don't know if I even want to.

I don't want to believe this is actually happening, but the man coming straight for me is as real as the glittering imperial crown proudly sitting in the display case next to my body, and just as filthy rich. He oozes confidence - that infuriating confidence that comes so naturally to him and which made me fall so heavily *and wrongly* for him the first time.

He was my first love.

My only love.

The man I could not – *can not* - resist.

He smiles at me in that devious way that has made my body instantly freeze in both terror and lust. Oh, how I remember that bewitching smile.

A ghost from my past.

Is it too late? Do I stay? Do I go?

What the hell do I do?

I gulp.

And then he speaks.

His words stab into my heart like a dagger, and I know that there's now absolutely zero chance of escape.

"Hello, *Queen*."

PROLOGUE

I'm STANDING by the Crown Jewels of the United Kingdom when I see *him* walking towards me, and I can't do shit.

The last time I saw him, he was just a boy, but now he is most definitely a man. All six-foot-two of him. Dressed elegantly in an expensive suit with his perfectly cut hair and that irresistible chiseled jaw I remember so vividly.

The man I thought I would never see again is walking towards me. The man that I *hoped* I would never see again is making his way across the room. In my direction.

The man I hate is coming for me, and I have no way to escape.

The man who made my teenage self cry into my pillow for endless heartbreaking nights.

I thought he was gone forever. Ripped from me in one cruel stroke. A decision to leave that he had made, and that I had no control over. I had felt such a fool back then to let him so easily tear my heart to shreds.

I had made a promise to myself if I saw him again that I would run in the opposite direction.

But right now, I'm not running.

FOUR YEARS EARLIER

KINGSLEY

I was the new boy.

And not only was I new, but I was also *foreign*. The British boy at an all-American high school. Our two countries might've spoken the same language, but you couldn't get any more different than that, trust me.

Staring out at my new high school, I sighed deeply and leaned back into the plush leather seat of the limousine. I turned my head from the window to Camilla in the front seat.

"I guess this is it," I said to her, nodding towards the cluster of brick buildings that made up the American high school I was to spend the next few months studying in.

Camilla – my so-called "adult guardian" - spun around in her car seat to look at me with her infamous ice-cold stare. Next to her, the American driver kept absolutely still.

Camilla gave off a sort of strict British headmistress air that frightened most people into quivering submission, including the poor limousine driver my father had hired to take us around this small town.

Not me, though. I'd known Camilla all my life. I was not scared of her steely presence. Well, not most of the time.

"Yes, King. Here we are," Camilla replied as she pulled out a pair of dark sunglasses, placing them delicately over her eyes as if to protect herself from America itself. She looked outside the window at the streams of students rushing around in front of the high school. It was like a scene out of any Hollywood coming-of-age film. Real *John Hughes* type stuff. Yellow buses and jocks dressed in jerseys. Cheerleaders and skateboarders. "It's an absolute shame that America is so full of *Americans*."

"Please, Camilla. Tell me how you really feel. Don't hold back."

"Trust me, King, if it was up to me, I wouldn't be here in this country," my adult guardian replied sternly. "Not in a million years. Very tacky place, this is. Very loud, the lot of them."

"They're not too bad, Camilla."

"Oh yes, they are. And what is the deal with their chocolate? It is absolutely disgusting."

I had to laugh. I loved Camilla. She always reminded me of a snarky Helen Mirren, although I would never dare tell her that; she wasn't good with comparisons or pop culture. She wouldn't even know who Helen Mirren was. She had that dry and witty English personality in spades but behind that cold exterior, she could be playful. You just had to know how to bring it out of her.

And I was one of the only people who could.

"I'm glad Father forced you to accompany me here with

female student outside the front doors would not go down well, I reckoned.

I noticed the shy, beautiful girl was holding something in between her hands and her chest. Something big and bulky. Heavy. A book of some sort. I squinted my eyes to have a better look at it. I could make out one word printed on the front cover.

Shakespeare.

I chuckled to myself. She was *actually* carrying the entire works of the Elizabethan playwright into school? All those pages? Was she crazy?

It was cute, though.

She must've been no older than I was. Eighteen. We were probably in the same year. We'll probably meet in the next few days.

Ah.

That would be interesting.

"So, are you going to go in?" Camilla asked me, impatient for me to leave the limo.

"Just getting my bag."

I continued to watch the redhead as she glided into school. I did not lose her in the crowd. She stopped by the entrance and started a conversation with an adult. Presumably a teacher. As she spoke, she avoided eye contact with the man. She bit her lip as he spoke to her about something serious.

She really doesn't know how beautiful she really is, does she?

Had no other guy picked up on that? Had she a boyfriend? Some guy who treated her like the beauty she was?

Slowly, the girl tucked a lock of her red hair behind her ear. I smiled.

I'd seen enough.

I leaned forward again and pulled up my bag.

"Right," I announced. "I'm going in. Wish me luck."

"Good luck, King. Have a good first day."

Camilla smiled at me. Actually *smiled* at me.

"Wow, genuine sincerity coming from you? That's rare, Camilla."

Her smile reverted back to her usual steel expression. "Don't get used to it. These bloody Yanks and their bloody emotions are rubbing off on me. I'll be sure to put a stop to that immediately."

I laughed and leaped out of the car. Into my new school.

I searched the crowd of students lingering outside the front doors for the girl with the red hair, but she was gone. She was probably deep within the high school now.

But that was no problem. I was sure I'd run into her again.

For sure I will. I have a mission now.

I might have been the new boy stepping onto unknown ground here in a foreign country, but I did know one thing.

I must have her.

2

SCARLETT

WHY DO boys love sports so much? Maybe I'm just a "fragile emotional and physically weak female" – that's according to a guy called Mick in my class when I spoke to him about it once - but I just don't get boys' obsession over throwing an inflated ball around.

I'm not a sporty girl. Sure, I like to jog and generally keep active, but it's not like I'm going to be eagerly rushing out to play football every free moment I have. But here, at Crystal River High, it seems like every single boy just can't wait to get their hands around a football or to tackle another thick-headed male on the field. Like it's a drug they can't get enough of.

I mean, each to their own, but personally I would much rather spend my free time reading than wrestling other people in the mud.

And that was what I was doing that day when I spoke to *him* for the first time. Sitting on the bleachers by Crystal River High's football field, reading a battered copy of *Pride and Prejudice.* I was reading the courtship of Miss. Elizabeth Bennet and the dashing Mr. Darcy as the boys of my school year were busy chasing after a football only a few yards away. Maybe boys couldn't understand my love of Jane Austen in the same way I didn't understand their love for sports.

As I read, I tied my red hair into a ponytail so that it wouldn't blow in the restless wind.

I was alone. I preferred it that way. It meant I could enjoy the book in peace. I could just sit there on the bleachers and get deeply lost in Regency England and forget all about small town America. I could dream about a fantasy world where men were actually gentlemen. Where they could sweep you off your feet at a fancy ball. Where love was conducted through long flowery letters sent across the country. Where men dressed in handsome suits and women wore elegant dresses. A world where there was no NFL or sports or high school.

If you spoke to any one of my family members or friends, they would all say I dreamed about that fantasy world a little *too* much. I couldn't disagree. My head was always in the clouds, daydreaming of other worlds. That was probably why I loved theater so much. Plays. Novels. Things that were set in places other than Crystal High in middle-of-nowhere America. I wanted to see those worlds. I wanted to travel. I wanted to get out of my small town.

And there was one place in the real world I wanted to go to above all others.

London.

The place where theater is. The place Jane Austen wrote about. Where Shakespeare scribbled and performed. A big city far away from Crystal River. That's where I wanted to live.

I closed my book and looked out over the football field.

The boys-who-definitely-weren't-Mr.-Darcy scurried around like ants in the distance chasing after a football.

London would be very different from this place.

The sound of voices brought me back to reality. Sitting further down the bleachers was a group of girls. The popular girls of Crystal River High. I noticed Lisa Cartwright in the middle. She was, by far, the prettiest girl in my school year. And, boy, did she know it. She was the queen bee of Crystal River High. The head cheerleader. The girl every guy wanted to date, and every girl wanted to be friends with.

She and her gaggle of friends all sat around on the bleachers, watching and gossiping about the boys playing. They weren't exactly being quiet. I wasn't into high school social politics at all, but I couldn't help but overhear their conversation.

Okay, so maybe I was a *teeny tiny* bit interested in what they were saying.

"I reckon Justin's gay," one girl announced to the group.

"No way. He can't be gay," Lisa interrupted with the easy confidence of a leader, flicking her luscious blonde hair back over her shoulder. "I know, for a fact, that Anne Winter gave him a blowjob literally the other week in his car."

"Oh my god. How do you know?"

"She told me."

"Wow. She said that to you?"

"Yeah," Lisa continued. "She's such a slut."

They caught sight of me watching them.

"What you doing?" Lisa asked me, calling out in an accusatory voice across the bleachers. "Being a creep, I bet?"

I lifted up my copy of *Pride and Prejudice* towards her.

"Not much creeping today," I replied. "I'm just reading."

Lisa snorted and pulled a disgusted face. "Nerd."

She turned back to the other schoolgirls and giggled. I sighed.

Soon they had forgotten all about me. They were all gossiping about the boys in the year. A topic they had touched on at least once every hour for the past four years.

"What do you think of the new boy?" asked one of Lisa's minions.

Lisa paused at the question. I watched her bite her lower lip, thinking. The other girls leaned over to hear her answer. The question of the new boy was definitely a hot topic, and the whole school was awaiting the judgment of its queen bee.

"I am *obsessed*," Lisa replied dramatically.

The other girls squealed in agreement. Judgment delivered.

"I heard he's British," one cheerleader said.

"*English*," Lisa corrected as if she knew all about the United Kingdom. "And he's got the accent. Yum."

I knew who they were talking about. The new hot British boy was the talk of the school that day. I actually had him in one of my classes earlier. Theater class. I had a good look at him then.

He definitely was hot, and that was putting it mildly. He was tall, at least six feet. Broad-shouldered. Smooth skin and a sculptured jawline straight out of a model catalog. His cheekbones were sharp, like they were cut from marble. His face oozed confidence. His soft lips seemed to be permanently formed into a slight smirk, as if he were above us always looking down. It didn't seem like he was from this world.

Of course, he didn't speak to me. No one of his status would acknowledge the bookish girl sitting alone in the corner.

He didn't even wear the normal attire of an American schoolboy. He wore a casual suit. No tie. The top button was undone, showing a glimpse of a muscular chest. I didn't know much about suits, but even I could tell the outfit was expensive. I had never seen a boy at school wear a suit like that. No American boy would even dare attempt that attire.

Dark and mysterious, the new boy didn't say a single word the entire lesson. He just sat back and observed everyone in the class with his penetrating blue eyes like he was in a zoo and we were all the monkeys behind the glass throwing our shit around.

But there was something delicate about him as well. The way he moved. He wasn't brash or eager to prove himself like other boys my age were. He glided through the school with a self-assuredness that didn't require big bravado. He clearly didn't care what others thought of him.

The devil in a suit. That's who he is.

"He's going to be mine," Lisa Cartwright told the girls. "I want a British boy."

She reminded me of a lioness stalking her prey.

"Good luck, British boy," I said under my breath.

Poor guy. Lisa is like a terminator when it comes to fresh, handsome blood.

He was out there on the field, playing football with the other boys. I turned from the popular girls and towards the field. I found him amongst the players. It wasn't hard; he was the tallest by far. One of the most muscular. He moved with the football in the same way he flew down the high school hallways. Cool and confident. Like everything came super easy to him.

No wonder Lisa and the popular girls fancied a shot at him.

I don't blame them at all.

He was certainly not in my league, that was for sure. I

was just the bookish girl of Crystal River High who was into plays. No way could I land a boy like that.

I glanced down at my copy of *Pride and Prejudice* and sighed again. I would just have to forget about the real British boy who went to my school and go back to reading about a fictional one.

Suddenly – as I turned the page in my book - a noise startled me. It was a yell.

It was coming from the field.

I looked up from my book to see a terrifying sight.

A football was hurtling at top speed. In the air.

Directly towards me.

And it was too late to dodge.

3

SCARLETT

THE SPINNING FOOTBALL was on a direct collision course for my face.

And it was too late to get out of the way. So I did what any self-respecting strong woman would do.

I tightly shut my eyes and let out a high-pitched squeal.

But in the next few moments, I felt no pain. The football had not hit me.

Confused, I opened my eyes to see the thing caught mid-air by a boy. And not just any boy.

The new British student.

I blinked. Shocked.

In order to catch the football, the British boy's arm was stretched out far, showing his thick bicep. He was no longer dressed in that expensive suit he was wearing earlier in the day, now he was in top-brand sportswear. I tried, and failed, to avoid glancing down at the designer shorts that were a bit too tight around his perfectly formed ass.

Damn. He really knew how to wear clothes.

From the other side of the bleachers, Lisa Cartwright and the rest of the popular girls were just staring at us.

I did not move. My mouth still hung open from my scream. I reminded myself to close it.

The British boy slowly turned his head towards me and winked. He pulled in the football to his chest and held it strongly between his biceps.

Jesus Christ.

"Saved you," he said to me. His voice was deep and melodious. An English accent that was like cut glass.

"Um... thanks."

I couldn't think of anything better or wittier to say. Surely, Elizabeth Bennet would've replied with something sharp, but not me. Not Scarlett Hart. I just stuttered out a pathetic reply.

"You okay?" he asked.

"I think I am."

He nodded. "Good to hear."

My God, that accent...

"Hey, King!"

One of the other boys on the field rushed towards the bleachers, waving his arm.

The British boy seemed to know what the other boy wanted. He leaned back his muscular arm and easily threw the football across the field towards the waiting boy. I was expecting him to disappear then, for that short and awkward exchange to be our only interaction.

But the British boy didn't run back to be with the rest of the players. He just turned back around to me, smiling.

There was something in that smile. A deep intelligence. I'd never seen a boy smile like that before. Confident. He was not after anything, but he stared at me with an intense focus. Like a predator. Someone who played by his own rules.

We settled into an awkward silence. Him standing there at the front of the bleachers, me sitting down with my copy of *Pride and Prejudice* resting on my lap and not knowing what to do. My mind was totally blank. It was like he was waiting for me to say something, but I couldn't think of what to say.

The way he looked at me with his dark, smoldering gaze made me blush. Hard. It was the only thing I could do. I mean, the boy was hot. Like, *flaming* hot. I was horny. And he had just saved me from an embarrassing and painful hit.

And yet I resolved not to swoon over him like some love-struck virgin, no matter how much his perfect face made the insides of my body tumble about. As I've said, he was way above me in high school status. I was – in Lisa Cartwright's eloquent terms – the creepy bookish girl. Not the kind of person this guy would be interested in at all.

But he was still standing there. Looking at me.

"Good book?" the British boy eventually asked, nodding at my lap.

I blinked again and looked down at the paperback.

Oh, right. He's talking about that.

"Yeah, it is."

Another witty reply, Scarlett. Be careful not to overwhelm him with your social graces.

"I saw you earlier," he said. His accent was so strong and playful that it had me spinning. Sweat dripped from his unkempt hair. *Sexy.*

"Oh, okay. You were staring at me?"

He chuckled quietly. "I wouldn't call it staring. When I *saw* you, you were carrying the complete works of Shakespeare."

Right. That. "Yes, I was. I like to read his stuff."

His stuff? Wow, slow down with those zingers, Scarlett.

The British boy chuckled again. "I've never seen anyone

carrying around the entire works, let alone into high school. It must be pretty heavy."

I pointed at my schoolbag. "I have space. I can carry things."

I can carry things? What are you even saying, doofus?

"I see that," the British boy replied. "You can carry things."

Was he being serious or sarcastic? I couldn't tell with that accent.

"Are you mocking me?" I asked him.

The British boy seemed taken aback by that. His smile quickly morphed into a frown.

"Do you think I'm mocking you?"

"I'm getting that impression."

"You mind if I sit next to you?"

Without even waiting for my reply, he leaped up onto the bleachers athletically and helped himself to the spot next to me. I felt his sweaty shirt brush against my leg. I quivered at his touch.

"What do you want?" I asked softly. I didn't know what he was doing. Why was he sitting next to me?

"I want to be an actor," he said. "That's why I asked about you carrying Shakespeare. I would love to perform one of his plays one day."

"Oh," I replied. "You want to be an actor. Like, on stage and screen performing and stuff?"

"That's what actors usually do, isn't it?"

I rolled my eyes at him. "You know, that's actually pretty cool."

I meant it.

"You're in my Theater class, right?" he asked me. "I think I saw you there earlier."

"Yeah, I am," I said. "Though I'm terrible at it. I don't

think I'm a good actor at all. I go because I like Shakespeare and the theater."

"Don't be so hard on yourself. I'm sure you're bloody terrific at acting."

I giggled at his British slang.

"Trust me, you haven't seen me act," I replied. "Or sing. My voice will blow your eardrum."

I was nervous. He seemed so big next to me, with his broad shoulders and bulging biceps. I was the bookish girl, and he was the boy every girl was talking about. We shouldn't have been sitting together, and especially not this close.

I was normally like this around new people. Shy, I mean. I sometimes found it hard to talk to complete strangers, and that would make me come across as snarky. I resented that horrible side of myself. I would've thought that my involuntary curtness would throw the British boy off from me, but apparently, he did not care at all and wanted to continue talking. That was the crazy thing.

He actually wanted to keep talking to the weird book girl with the spikey attitude.

"I'm sure my eardrums won't blow," the British boy replied. He offered out his hand towards me. "I'm Kingsley. Kingsley Heath-Harding."

Oh, a double-barreled name? He must be posh. That would explain the limo.

I shook his hand. "Scarlett. Scarlett Hart."

His strong grip calmed my nerves. His hand was warm. He must've been working out hard on the football field to build up such a sweat.

I felt the eyes of Lisa Cartwright burn into me from across the bleachers.

"Nice name," he said.

"Thanks."

"My name is Kingsley, but everyone calls me King."

I snorted with laughter. I couldn't help myself. "*King?*"

"What's wrong?"

"Nothing. It's just... a very *strong* nickname."

"Well, I like it. Call me King."

"I'm not calling you King," I replied. "I'll call you Kingsley. Your real name."

He elbowed me playfully in the ribs. "Oh, come on. Call me King."

I elbowed him back. "It's cheesy."

Are we... flirting?

"No, it isn't."

"I'll call you Kingsley, Kingsley."

"Fine, Scarlett Hart," he replied. "I'll let you call me that, but only you."

"Thank you for the honor."

"My pleasure."

I nodded towards the football field. "I guess you don't play our kind of football back home?"

"No, we play *proper* football."

"What's it been like?"

"Playing American football?"

"Yeah."

"Well, it's nothing like English football. That's for sure."

"No, it isn't," I replied. "American football is all big dudes, and your football is full of pretty men with nice haircuts."

Kingsley pulled a face at me. "Is this a roundabout way for you to call me pretty, Scarlett Hart?"

I bit my lip in embarrassment. I did not mean that. "Nope."

Kingsley leaned in close. His muscular shoulder brushed up against mine. "Sounds like you are."

"No, I wasn't."

"By the look on your face, I'm taking it as you are calling me pretty."

He was putting me completely at ease, despite my awkwardness. He was easy to talk to.

And it's very easy to get lost in his blue eyes.

"That reminds me. There was something I was going to say to you," he said. "When I first saw you earlier today."

"When you were staring at me?"

"Kind of."

"What is it?" I asked.

He shook his head as if he was embarrassed at himself.

"Nothing. It was nothing. Forget it."

"Go on, tell me. I'm curious now."

To have been not only noticed by a boy but to have him want to *say* something secretive to me put all my senses on edge.

"You would just think I'm silly," he replied.

"Believe me, I wouldn't."

"Where are you from, Scarlett?"

He wanted to change the subject. Okay, then.

"I'm from here. Crystal River. Middle of nowhere."

"I wouldn't say nowhere," he replied. "This town is nice."

"Nice? This is just like any number of a thousand towns in this country."

"Don't talk ill of either yourself or where you come from," Kingsley said quietly. "Be proud of who you are. You may think this place is another one of thousands, but there is nothing else in the world like home. There is nobody else in the world like you."

My heart skipped a beat.

Was he talking about me? Or just people in general?

Obviously in general, Scarlett. No way could he be saying you're special. He doesn't even know you.

"That's a very sincere speech," I told him.

"I've practiced it lots of times. You think it came out alright?"

He was funny, I'd give him that. I felt like I could talk to him for the rest of the school day.

But then, right on cue, another boy shouted across the football field.

"King!"

Kingsley looked up and waved at the boy. He turned back to me.

"I better head back out. It was nice meeting you, Scarlett."

"It was nice meeting you, Kingsley."

"You're never going to call me King, aren't you?"

I grinned at him. I must've looked like a right dork, but he seemed to like it.

"Never."

"Right. See you."

He leaped back down the bleachers, jumping a step in a single bound.

But before he ran back onto the field, he turned back to me.

"You must allow me to tell you how ardently I admire and love you," he said.

What.

My heart seemed to stop beating with his unexpected words.

"Excuse me?" I stammered.

Kingsley nodded at my lap again. "It's from *Pride and Prejudice*. Mr. Darcy says it. I guess you're not up to that bit yet."

I smiled and shook my head, catching onto what he was meaning. "No, I'm not."

"They do get together in the end. I hope that didn't spoil it for you."

Kingsley winked again and dashed off back to the football game.

I sat completely still for a moment, trying to come to grips with what had just happened. That interaction. I didn't know how to process it.

Kingsley Heath-Harding was just so... *overwhelming*. So full of strength, but there was also a gentleness in which he looked at me. The way he gently teased me. Made me feel at ease.

Or maybe I was just overthinking it. Typical me. The girl with fiction running on a loop in her head, falling instantly in love with the first British man she sees.

I shuffled in my seat on the bleachers, catching a glance of Lisa and her gang. I realized then that they hadn't stopped looking in my direction since Kingsley had caught the football.

And now they were all staring at me with murder in their eyes.

4

KINGSLEY

GRAVEL CRUNCHED under the tires as the limo drove up to the mansion Father had rented for Camilla and me during our stay in America.

As I stepped out of the vehicle, I looked up and down the impressive building. Four stories tall, it housed a private gym, pool, and tennis court. Just for us two. A suitable home-away-from-home for any young English aristocrat.

Father got the place specifically because it was the most expensive property to rent in the whole of Crystal River. Even on the other side of the world, Lord Heath-Harding liked to flaunt his wealth.

I thanked the limo driver and stepped inside the mansion to be greeted with the beautiful and intoxicating smell of beef roast.

"The smell of home," I muttered.

I headed straight for the source, directly into the kitchen. Camilla was at the counter, an apron tied around her waist. She was cooking.

She glanced up at me as I entered.

"I couldn't bear it any longer," she announced with her perfect diction. "I just had to make a roast. I couldn't stand any more of this sugary Yank food any longer."

I gave her a quick peck on the cheek. "Of course you couldn't. It smells delicious, Camilla."

"Sit down. I'll be serving it in a moment."

She didn't need to tell me twice. I dashed to the dining table that was already laid out for me. Camilla was a seasoned pro at running a household.

"How was your day?" I asked her.

Camilla waved her hand dismissively. "I don't give a toss about my day," she said. "I want to hear about yours. I am so curious. How was your first day at an American high school? Was it *awesome*?"

Yep. She really tried an American accent on the word *awesome*. Just to prove how much she detested American slang.

I laughed. "It truly was *awesome*. Played football. Did some classes. It really is just like the movies."

Camilla rolled her eyes. "Oh, how wonderful."

"Come on, Camilla. Drop your dry wit for once. It's not all bad."

"Oh yes, it is."

"America?"

"Well, it's not exactly London, is it? It's as bad as I imagined."

"But don't you want to experience new things? Have new adventures in a foreign country?"

She raised a spatula threateningly towards me. "King, I am an elderly woman. I have had enough adventures in my life, thank you very much. I can assure you that Crystal River is not one of them."

Now it was my turn to roll my eyes. "You know why we're here, though, don't you?"

"Yes."

"Father is very keen on me going to Harvard. A few months in an American high school will help me acclimatize to this country. Make it easier for me to fit in there. Well, that's what he says, anyway."

Earlier that day, I had been approached – well, apprehended – in the high school hallway by an obnoxious cheerleader. She was the very stereotype of the all-American girl. Blonde hair. Perfect teeth. I knew what she was immediately by the way her eyes traveled down over my body and by the way she jutted forward her tits.

"Hi, I'm Lisa," she said in a cheerful American accent.

Here goes. Help me, Lord.

"King."

A girl like her would be fun. For a night. For a quick and easy lay. But there was certainly no depth to her. Nothing to keep me interested beyond getting my dick wet.

Lisa bit her plump lower lip and sighed at me as I said my name. American chicks and the way they fawned over my accent. It was starting to get really tiresome. "You're new here, aren't you?"

She was eyeing me like I was another trophy for her to collect. Her stare wandered down to my crotch, but my cock was in no way hard for her. I hated it when girls went all *gaga* over me. I knew I could say anything I wanted to this superficial girl. Make her do anything I wanted, and she would.

But she was not the girl I wanted to control.

"Yep."

"Well, I practically *know* this school and this town more than anyone here. How about I be your tour guide?"

"I have no need for one," I replied. "But thank you for your kind offer."

And then I turned and walked away from her. I heard a loud harrumph from behind me as I head down the hallway. The Lisa girl had clearly not experienced rejection before.

But a ditzy cheerleader like her held no interest for me. No. I was after someone more challenging. The shy girl with the entire works of Shakespeare who had dominated my thoughts all day.

Up close, she did not disappoint. She was even more beautiful sitting there on the bleachers than when I spotted her in the morning. That cascading red hair turned me on. And she was reading *Pride and Prejudice*, my kind of book. When I sat next to her, I spied the curve of her breasts. Fuck me, I thought. She was trying to self-consciously hide her body, but she had absolutely no need to. The sight of her body made my cock hard. I wondered what it would be like to squeeze those hidden tits. To make her moan uninhibited. I was going crazy over her.

If only she knew.

I doubt she did. She seemed nervous to even talk to me, but there was a little spark in her. Something that liked to bite back. A little bit of Elizabeth Bennet in her. The way she refused to call me by my "cheesy" nickname and instead by my full one, *that* spicy attitude was sexy as hell. I liked a girl that didn't give me what I wanted or tried to seduce me for status like that Lisa. I liked a girl that made me fight for her affection.

Camilla brought over two plates of roast beef to the dining table, both covered in thick gravy. With even a Yorkshire pudding on top. My favorite.

"Bon appétit," she said triumphantly.

"How on earth did you find a Yorkshire pudding in this country?" I asked in bewilderment.

Camilla winked at me devilishly. "Oh, I may be an elderly woman, but I do have my ways, King. I know a few people."

"You're like a drug dealer if they existed in Downton Abbey."

"I will take that as a compliment. Yorkshire puddings are hard to find in small town America."

"You know, every day you amaze me, Camilla."

She sat opposite me but didn't start eating. She just stared at me as I tucked in.

"Do you even want to go to Harvard, King?" she eventually asked as I was putting a thick slice of beef into my mouth.

"Blimey," I replied, dropping the beef back onto my plate. "That's a deep and very random question."

"It really isn't. Do you want to go or is it just your father's wishes? Because if not, then why come halfway across the world for no reason?"

I tutted, trying to avoid the topic. "Camilla, he's your employer. You can't say bad things about him."

"Oh, whatever. He can't fire me now. I've been around you lot for years. I've got all the dirt on your little family to ruin you lot."

"I don't doubt you do."

"But, seriously, do you want to go to Harvard?"

I placed my knife and fork down.

"I want to be an actor," I replied softly. "And I don't know if that's the sort of thing you go to Harvard for, but what Father says has to happen. You know that as well as anybody."

Camilla shook her head. "I thought as much. You know you don't have to do something just because your father says so. Even if he is a certified Lord. You are your own person."

"I know."

"I've watched you grow up, King. You're one of the most confident and talented young men I've ever come across. You don't seem beholden to no one, except for your father, but you can do anything you want."

There was a long pause at the dinner table. Things had gotten serious. Camilla was always sarcastic in her stiff upper-lip British kind of way, so to see her get deep like this was a very rare sight indeed.

She really did care for me.

"Your mother would've wanted you to pursue your passion," Camilla said softly. "No matter what your father would say."

I bowed my head, not wanting Camilla to see the emotion creeping up on me. Any mention of my mother, especially from someone who actually knew her as Camilla had once done, made me feel things I would've much preferred to have kept locked away. It was not my nature to get sentimental.

"I wouldn't know," I said. "I barely knew her."

"Well, she would've wanted you to do whatever makes you happy," Camilla quietly said. Slowly and deliberately, she reached forward over the table for my hand, clasping it in hers. It was a display of emotion I had never seen from her since the day of my mother's funeral all those years ago when I was a child. I remember that day Camilla wrapped her arms around me and held me tight for a very long time without speaking a word.

We'd never spoken about that moment since. It's not what us upper-class British people do. We suppress our emotions and just *get on* with living. No dilly dallying with such American things as *emotions*.

And I especially didn't want to talk about my mother. Memories of her were a fading thing for me. She passed when I was just a boy, and I didn't remember much of her.

Please not now.

As if on cue, the minute Camilla's hand touched mine, my phone started to loudly ring. Perfect timing.

Saved by the bell.

I jumped out of the seat, away from Camilla, and pulled out my phone. My brother's name flashed up on the screen.

Duke.

I knew he was calling to check up on me. Doing the elder brother duties, I guess.

I gestured to Camilla that I was going to take the call and headed upstairs to my room.

"Hello, Duke."

"King."

"How're things? How's London?"

"Raining. As usual."

Out of the both of us, my brother was known as the quiet one. Girls always loved him because he was so dark and brooding. They flocked to his silent nature, and he pushed them away just as easily. I guessed that girls loved me because I was the charming one of the two. We both had our strengths, and we played to them well.

Not to brag, but there was a lot of physical evidence to back it up. Not that I kept any of the unsolicited nudes that girls sent me. I was still an English gentleman of good breeding.

"Typical London," I replied to my brother. I was glad to hear his voice, although I would never admit it to him. "I miss the rain, though. How's Father?"

"Silent. As usual."

"Of course."

My brother scoffed. "And how's America? Is it like Disney World on crack?"

"In some ways, it is. High school's fun, though."

"Really?"

I could practically *hear* my brother's raised eyebrow down the phone.

"It really is fun. They have aisles in the supermarket specially devoted to just cereal."

"Sounds exhausting," he replied.

"Oh, it's great. Everything's just so... *big* here."

"And how are the high school classes?"

"Well. They are a bit behind over here compared to our old boarding school. For one thing, no one knows any Latin or Ancient Greek."

Even though my boarding school back home was only for boys, I definitely knew how to pleasure a girl. How to make them squirm. I wondered what expression little Miss Hart's pretty face would have if I were to touch her right where I wanted.

The thought made my cock hard, even on a phone call with my brother.

"That's a shame. And the girls? How are they? As stuck-up as English ones?"

That was so typical Duke. Straight to the pussy. There was no girl I'd ever met who was immune to Duke's flirty bullshit.

"What you'd expect to find in a place like this. Cheer-leaders and the like."

"And have you found anyone that catches your eye? A pretty little American girl?"

I laughed but didn't reply.

"I'm taking that as a *yes*, King."

"Shut up and go make some more bags of money or whatever it is you do," I replied, rolling my eyes.

The line went dead. My brother was good at cutting things off.

And I didn't want to answer his question.

All I could think of was the girl I saved from the football. The shy girl with fiery red hair. The wannabe Miss. Elizabeth Bennet.

The girl who so mockingly refused to call me by my nickname. Her refusal both infuriated and aroused me. I could tell that this girl who shied away had an inner steel underneath, and I wanted to be the boy who brought it out of her. Properly.

I didn't have long to wait for her, though. I had Theater class tomorrow.

I'd be seeing her then.

5

SCARLETT

I SPRINTED down the empty high school hallways, clutching my bulky textbooks against my chest so tight that they crushed my boobs. I didn't care, though; I was too busy praying to whatever gods there might be up there that I wasn't going to be late.

But I knew that I was.

My lateness wasn't my fault. Well, it *kinda* wasn't. My phone didn't go off that morning, okay? For whatever reason, it just didn't.

I'm usually one of those annoying people that sets, like, six alarms to go off every minute after my intended wake-up time. But on that particular night, I had set only one.

And it didn't go off. So, *technically*, it wasn't my fault.

Although it really was.

My excuses didn't matter, though. I was still late for Theater class.

I finally made it to the rehearsal room, sweating and hot. A total mess.

With a big gulp of air, I opened the door and stepped inside the room.

As I expected, the class was already in session, and everyone's head immediately turned to face me as the door swung open. I felt all their curious eyes falling on me, and my sweaty ass, at once. I knew what they were thinking. Judging the late girl panting like a dog.

And all I wanted to do was curl up in a ball and hide away.

"Um, hi," I awkwardly greeted no one in particular as I tiptoed in, finding my regular spot at the back of the class.

"You're late," the theater teacher, Mrs. Stone, said. As if I didn't know that.

"Sorry."

This is a total nightmare. Everyone's looking at the shy girl. I can't handle it.

She nodded at me and turned back to the class. Their eyes turned with her, and I was thankful I was no longer the center of attention.

I sat down near one of my friends, Liv. She smiled at me sweetly. She was a good friend. We always paired up for theater assignments.

As Mrs. Stone gave a lecture about Brechtian techniques in modern theater, I organized my textbooks and tried to steady my breathing. I glanced around the room, happy to see no one looking at me from my safe space all the way at the back.

That was, until I noticed Kingsley.

He was staring at me with his deep blue eyes from across the room. Unblinking. He was laser-focused on me, but he didn't say anything.

My whole body shuddered involuntarily at his gaze, and I quickly averted my eyes back down to my scattered textbooks on the ground.

I had completely forgotten he was in my Theater class. And now he had seen me like this. Sweaty and ugly.

Ugh.

I tried to resist the urge to look back up again. I failed.

He was no longer staring at me, but that still didn't help evaporate the feeling of being watched by him.

Did I really look that horrible after my desperate run through the school to warrant such a stare? Or was there something else to him looking at me from across the room? I couldn't tell. The British boy was an enigma to me ever since he casually sat down close to me on those bleachers yesterday and quoted Jane Austen to my face.

I couldn't help noticing other girls in the class peeking over at him as well. Was he really that irresistible to females? He obviously was.

I shook my head and tried to ignore him. As Mrs. Stone continued talking, Liv shuffled up close to me.

"Have you seen the new boy?" she asked, her voice a whisper so the teacher couldn't hear.

I nodded.

Please not this conversation. Anything but this conversation.

"He's cute, isn't he?"

"Not you too," I replied. "It seems like everyone in this school has gone *gaga* over him."

"Can you blame them?"

I smiled and shook my head. I definitely couldn't blame them.

Mrs. Stone finished her speech and was now talking about assignments.

"Okay, so we're going back to basics with this one," she told the class. "I'm going to pair you all up and then I want each pair to perform a scene from a play. Easy enough, right?"

Liv raised her hand. "Can we get to choose the scene?"

"No."

The whole class groaned.

"I'll choose the scene for you," Mrs. Stone continued. "Each pair will get a different one, and it will be from a *classical* play."

Another, even louder, groan erupted.

Mrs. Stone set about pairing up students from a list. Liv and I looked at each other, hoping we'd be put together like all the other times we've had to do something like this.

But it wasn't going to be. Mrs. Stone set Liv with another girl.

And then she said my name.

And my partner's.

My body went rigid when I heard his name.

"Kingsley."

"Actually, it's *King*," the British boy announced with his charming smile.

The teacher giggled at his correction like a nervous schoolgirl. I had never seen her giggle before. Was she... *flirting* with him? "Oh, sorry. King. You and Scarlett are to pair up."

"Perfect," Kingsley replied, picking up his books and making his way directly over to me.

I tried to swallow, but there was a lump in my throat.

"Hello, you," Kingsley said as he sat down next to me. "Pride and Prejudice girl."

"What scene do you want us to do?" I asked the teacher, trying to keep my eyes away from the tall boy brushing up against me.

"This one." She handed us both a sheet of paper. The lump in my throat seemed to grow ten times bigger the moment I read the title.

Romeo and Juliet.

"Perfect," Kingsley repeated as he read the sheet.

"You want us to perform this scene together?" I asked Mrs. Stone.

"Yes. On Monday. I trust I can leave it up to you all to rehearse these on your own."

She strolled over to her desk, leaving me alone with Kingsley.

I glanced back down at the script. The scene we had to do was the first meeting between the two lovers. I knew it well, and so, it seemed, did Kingsley.

"Oh, this is going to be fun," he said with glee. "*My lips, two blushing pilgrims, ready stand to smooth that rough touch with a tender kiss.*"

Great. He was already quoting it.

"Yeah, I like it too," I said, trying hard not to seem like I was freaking out. "It'll be good."

Kingsley's blue eyes, under his dark fringe, seemed to pierce me.

How was I going to do this? How could I hold myself together?

I decided to talk about anything other than the scene. Maybe I could find out more about this mysterious boy.

"You're popular with the girls," I said, nudging him in the direction of a pair on the other side of the room who were obviously whispering about him and not keeping it very subtle.

Kingsley scoffed and rolled his eyes. "Oh, I'm *so* popular and I *love* it," he replied sarcastically. "They don't even know me. People care more about appearances than what's on the inside."

"Well, your appearance is certainly creating a stir. You know the entire female population of the school is talking about you?"

"Really?" he asked, interested. "What are they saying?"

"Oh, rumors," I replied, trying to keep it light. "You know. You are the new boy with a British accent. That's something very different in Crystal River."

"I'm sure it is."

"Are you from London?"

Kingsley smiled at my question. "You're trying to avoid talking about the scene, Scarlett. How about we rehearse it?"

"Now?"

Sweat started to build up again on the back of my neck. The thought of saying these words - with Kingsley - made me nervous.

"When else?"

RING.

The school bell. Signaling the end of the lesson.

Kingsley laughed and reached over to get his bag. "How about we rehearse this tonight?"

"What? After school?"

"Well, we do have to perform the scene on Monday," he replied. "When else are we going to have the chance?"

He was right. It was Friday.

"Um, okay."

Kingsley casually slung his bag over his shoulder. The other kids in the class started to rush around us, leaving the room. "How about at your house tonight? You've got no plans, yeah?"

I actually did have plans. I was going to be a total geek and start watching the BBC version of *Pride and Prejudice*. You know, the good one with Colin Firth in it and not the awful movie with Keira Knightley. I'd bought popcorn especially for it.

"Sure. I'm free."

"Perfect."

"But what about you?" I asked. "Don't you have plans? I'm sure a popular guy like you has a party or something to go to."

"I may be Mr. Popular," Kingsley replied. "But tonight, I'd rather be doing something with you."

6

SCARLETT

THE DOORBELL RANG and my heart stopped. There was only one person who could be outside my family's front door at that time.

Kingsley was there. At my house.

I rushed down the stairs so that I could be the first one to get to the door. No way in hell was I going to let one of my parents see the guy.

"I'll get it," I shouted out to the kitchen where my parents were. "It's just my friend."

I didn't want them to answer the door and find out my so-called *friend* was actually a six-foot British hunk.

Kingsley was standing there in front of my family's house. It was dark outside behind him. His eyes glittered in the porch light.

"Hello," he said in his smooth accent.

"Come in." I quickly ushered him inside and pointed him in the direction of my bedroom, terrified one of my parents would suddenly appear being all curious.

In the safety of my bedroom, we sat down on my bed. Kingsley admired my room in all its teenage girl glory. He smiled at my decorations. I had a poster of One Direction on one wall. It'd been there for years. A poster of Zac Efron was lovingly displayed on another wall.

Real teenage girl stuff.

"Shut up," I said to Kingsley, glaring. I shut the door.

He raised his arms in surrender. "I didn't say anything."

"I see you judging. Some of this stuff has been up on my walls for years, okay?"

"I wasn't judging. I was just thinking of how cool thirteen-year-old Scarlett must've been."

"Ha ha, very funny."

His eyes flickered over a poster of London that I had over my bed. It was a fancy black-and-white one of Big Ben with a double-decker bus passing by. Kingsley raised an eyebrow at me.

"London, hey?"

I shrugged, trying to act nonchalant. "Yeah, I like it."

"My hometown."

"Do you miss it?" I asked.

"I'm enjoying America."

"You're avoiding the question."

Kingsley rolled his eyes. "What do you want, a teary confession of homesickness?"

"That would be fun to witness from you."

"What do you mean?"

I gestured him up and down. "Well, you being so... big and tough."

"*Big and tough?*" Kingsley laughed.

I suddenly felt embarrassed. "Weird choice of words, I know."

"Yeah, they were."

He might've been dismissive about homesickness, but

there definitely was something empty behind his tough exterior. I could sense grief for something deeper inside him than just missing his country, but what was it?

He really wasn't like other boys I knew.

"Don't joke about homesickness, Kingsley," I said. "I'm sure you feel something under all your bravado."

He scoffed. "I'm descended from a line of Lords who once led armies and rode into battle on steeds, Scarlett. There's hardness written in my blood."

"Wait, did you *really* just say the word *steeds* in a non-ironic way?"

I made him laugh. A deep chuckle that made his cute dimples cave in. I smiled at my accomplishment. "Okay, that definitely was a wrong choice of word," he said.

"Why are you here, though?" I asked. "In Crystal River, of all places?"

"My father wants me to go to an Ivy League college, so he thought it'll be good for me to experience small town America for a few months."

"And how's it going?"

"Some of the people are nice, and *some* people refuse to use my nickname."

"They must be insufferable."

"It's all part of the experience."

I snorted. "Well, if you were looking for the very definition of *small town*, then you've come to the right place. God, I would prefer London to here. I would prefer *anywhere* to here."

"It's not that bad," Kingsley said.

I shook my head. "Yeah, it is."

"Have you ever been to London?" he asked me.

I sat down on the bed next to him. "Mom took me there once when I was super young. We saw the musical *Cats*. I don't remember much of the trip, but I do remember being scared out of my pants at all the actors in cat costumes singing. It was my first ever theater show."

Kingsley leaned forward, curious. "So, I'm guessing you like theater?"

"Yeah."

"In the same way you like *Pride and Prejudice*?"

I giggled. "I *love* theater. And... well, actually... I want to go and live in London one day."

I didn't know why I uttered those words out loud. No one else knew about my future dreams, not even my parents. No one in the whole universe knew that I wanted to live in London, but now Kingsley knew. The words just came out of my mouth. He was just so easy to talk to.

Oh, great. Blabbermouth.

He smiled as if he knew he was the only one privy to that information.

"That's a good idea. London is a cool place. If you ever rock up there, then give me a shout. I'll happily act as host."

I felt my cheeks blushing. "Thanks."

"I'm being serious. I would love to show you my hometown."

The blueness of his eyes burned into me.

"I know."

He leaped up from the bed, breaking the quiet tension between us.

"Alright, let's get started on this scene, shall we?"

"Sure."

I had already memorized the scene, on account of me having already memorized most of *Romeo and Juliet*.

"Wow, you know all the words," Kingsley remarked when we finished a quick read-through of the scene. I didn't even glance down at my script once. "How come?

"I used to read it a lot as a little girl."

"You must've loved it."

"Saying I loved the play would be a severe understatement, Kingsley."

He laughed and playfully nudged my shoulder with his hand. His touch sent shivers down my spine. "You really are crazy, Scarlett Hart."

"Says the guy who's spending his Friday evening in a girl's bedroom with One Direction posters on the wall."

"Oh, I can think of worse places to be."

"Yeah?"

"Especially when I get to have some fun with you."

"Fun? What do you mean?"

His eyes were really burning into me at this point. I gasped softly.

"I'm talking about the acting, Scarlett," he said.

"Oh. Right."

You idiot, Scarlett. Stop pining after him like a puppy.

"Let's do the scene again, but this time on our feet."

We performed the scene in the middle of my bedroom. The whole time I was so overwhelmed by his manly presence in my actual freaking *bedroom* that I nearly forgot my lines at multiple points. I stumbled over my words all the way to the end of the page.

"Let's do that again, but this time actually maybe take a breath?" he asked when we finished the scene. He was right; my face was a bright shade of red due to my holding in my breath the entire time. I really couldn't get over him standing there reciting Shakespeare's words in his cut-glass perfect accent.

And he was really good at acting.

"Okay."

"Take in a deep breath, Scarlett," he smoothly instructed me.

I obeyed, taking in a long and slow mouthful of air whilst he watched me.

I can do this. I can act with him. He's no big deal. Sure, he's incredibly handsome and charming, but that's totally fine. I can deal with that.

"You're really good at acting," I said, letting my thoughts fly out of my mouth. "You should go pro."

Kingsley smirked. He was being so calm whilst I was a whirlwind of nerves. "Thanks," he replied. "Now, let's do that again."

And we did. This time, I was much better. I was actually getting into character.

During the performance, Kingsley took a few steps towards me so that our mouths were so close. We were nearly kissing. I knew it was just him performing, but it felt so real. It felt like I could reach out with my lips and he wouldn't stop me.

For a moment, it felt like we weren't even acting and just about to kiss.

Holy shit, this is so hot.

"Wow, you're really good," Kingsley said when we finished, breaking the intimate spell between us. "See, you're not as bad at acting as you made out you were."

"Shut up, you."

"Let's do it one more time," Kingsley suggested. He took a few steps towards me again so that we were in the same position as during the scene. His wide chest loomed over me. My eyes were fixated on his soft, full lips only inches from mine. My breathing shallowed at his closeness. "And how about this time let's include the kiss at the end of the scene?"

I had completely forgotten about Shakespeare's little scene direction of Romeo kissing Juliet. I thought we'd just ignore it. I was sure Mrs. Stone wouldn't expect us to actually kiss in front of the class.

But now Kingsley was suggesting we do it.

Do it right now.

In the intimacy of my bedroom.

"Um, okay," I replied. "Sure."

Act as though it is nothing. It is just a stage direction, Scarlett. Nothing more.

We started to perform the scene again. I tried to get through the words, but the thought of the kiss was foremost in my mind. I could barely act with Kingsley being so close and his lips so ready.

I was hesitant the whole way through. He must've been able to tell how goddamn nervous I was.

And then we reached the end of the scene.

Romeo kisses Juliet.

Kingsley reached forward, cupping my chin between his fingers to bring my face up to his. I let him.

And then he kissed me. Softly at first, and then with a strong passion.

I wrapped my arms around his shoulders, feeling the thick muscles under his shirt. He held my face with a deep confidence. He leaned in, heightening and intensifying the kiss.

It was more than just a kiss; this was an embrace.

This was more than just a stage direction. It wasn't just acting.

It was real.

7

SCARLETT

"That was nice," I said when our lips departed from each other.

Kingsley paused. "That was *nice?*"

"Okay, second use of poor choice of words tonight," I replied, blushing. "Maybe I should just stop talking before I embarrass myself even more."

I could still taste him on my lips, but I couldn't feel the rest of my body. Paralysis. I still couldn't believe we had actually kissed at the end of the scene.

It was so incredibly hot.

Hold yourself together, Scarlett.

And now I didn't know what to do with myself. Do I kiss him again? Dare I risk poisoning a perfect moment with my inevitable awkwardness?

"No," Kingsley said, lightly lifting my trembling chin up with his hand and staring deep into my eyes. "You have nothing to be embarrassed about, you gorgeous little thing. It really was nice."

And then he kissed me. Again.

Well, I guess that answers my question.

I wrapped my arms even tighter around him so that I was gripping his muscular frame, not knowing where any of this unbridled passion was leading to. I guess I did not care in the slightest as to what was going to happen next. Everything inside me was on edge, wishing to just stay embedded in this moment. Forever.

Kingsley's hands hurriedly ran through my red hair as if he'd been desperately dreaming of touching it for a long time. Those same hungry hands soon found their way down my neck and to the sensitivity of my lower back. I involuntarily shivered at his tender touch as he traced his fingers over my skin.

Jesus Christ. A girl can only take so much.

And then, together, we pulled back from each other as if trying to slow down this moment. We were both wanting to relish in this fleeting second before we inevitably committed our bodies to each other. To the both of us, it felt like a juncture. Once we moved – once we kissed for a third time – we understood that all bets were off. Our futures would be forever linked by our actions as soon as our lips touched once more. For a while, we just stared at the other's face as we basked in this brief moment before we knew everything would change. Complete silence reigned between us.

But this silence wasn't uncomfortable. In fact, it was the absolute opposite. Desire lit up like a flame inside the pit of my stomach as Kingsley's deep blue eyes penetrated my own. Heat surged between my legs as I scanned the immaculate contours of his cheekbones. My god, his face was just perfect. Chiseled to the point of ideal excellence. His eyes burned as his sight devoured me. I felt so wanted by him. I had never been so wanted before. The male's unrestrained lust sent me over the edge, and it was like all my thoughts flew from my head.

I just had to have him.

"Do you want to sit down?" I asked him, nodding towards my bed. I tried to pull his hand down to follow me, but he didn't budge.

"Shh," he whispered, holding my face between his fingers. "Let me take control."

My heart leaped in my chest. It was beating a million times a minute as Kingsley gently pushed me towards the bed so that I was lying down with him standing over me like an emperor satisfyingly surveying his domain.

When he looked at me like that, it was like he penetrated all my defenses and stripped my soul raw. What could I even do when he could take control over my body with just a single look?

You've fallen for him already, Scarlett. You didn't even know him a few days ago, but now it's certain this man will either marry you or give you the worst heartbreak in the world.

His intense eyes sparkled in the dim light as he pushed me onto the bed. He was taking me in with his gaze. He was soaking in every inch of me as if I was the most beautiful thing he'd ever seen.

A bare minute ago, we were rehearsing a scene, and now I was giving in to his sensual grip.

"What do you want?" I asked the strong boy, my voice quivering with anticipation.

He didn't say a word. He didn't need to. I knew what he wanted. It was obvious in his face what he wanted with a searing passion.

Me.

As Kingsley stood over me, pinning my wrists to the bed, I could see directly into him. I could clearly see that he was so focused on me that nothing else existed for him except for my eyes. I gasped. I had never been desired like this before. I had never felt someone's attention on me in this kind of way.

It made me feel submissive. Especially as he was tightly gripping my hands above my head on the bed. I couldn't move from under him and it turned me on so much.

Kingsley slowly leaned forward towards my face with the confidence of a man who knew he had all the time in the world. His lips reached my ear, where he nibbled eagerly at it for a moment before he whispered.

"I want to *feel* you, Scarlett."

A moan involuntarily escaped my mouth.

"What we're doing is so wrong," I replied. "So wrong. My parents are downstairs. We were just meant to be rehearsing."

"Was that the only reason you invited me into your bedroom or did you have ulterior *sexual* motives, you devious girl?"

Damn. He had me there.

But this had just been a fantasy I had concocted; it was not meant to actually happen. An impossible daydream. A girl coming home from high school on the bus coming up with the most insane situation in her head.

But now it was real.

"My parents..."

"They're not going to come in, are they?"

"No. Not unless they hear... noises."

"Well, then. You're going to be a good girl and stay quiet then, aren't you?"

"Yes."

"You'll be my good girl, Scarlett?"

"I will be."

"You promise?"

"I promise."

"Otherwise, I'll just have to punish you, and I don't know how much of that you will be able to take before you're screaming my name."

"Kingsley," I whispered. I couldn't object anymore to his advances. The only thing I could do now was say his name over and over. "Kingsley."

As if sensing my submission, the boy began to kiss my neck. And that's when I really gave into him.

"I don't want you to be touched by other boys, you understand? I want you to be all mine," he said. "All mine. My good girl."

"Oh, I will be your good girl."

His lips grazed my skin downward until he reached the top of my breasts. He paused, and then let go of my wrists. My hand immediately went to ruffle through his black curly hair whilst his own hand traced down my arm towards my pants.

He was unbuttoning them before I had a moment to comprehend what he was doing.

"You like this?" he asked me as I felt my pants loosen. "You want me to do this?"

"Kingsley, you can do whatever you like right now," I gasped. "Anything. I am totally in your control. You have me."

His desire seemed to burn out from within him. "I like that I've made you succumb to me," he hissed.

"That I have."

"You did put up a hell of a fight, though."

"Well, I can't fight anymore, Kingsley. It's all too much for me to resist."

His fingers edged towards my entrance. I was so wet for him. So eager.

"You want me, don't you?" he asked.

I nodded, biting my lip. "Yes, please. I want you so bad."

"My good girl."

"Say that again."

"My *good* girl."

Fuck me.

"Yes."

His fingers entered me. I rolled my eyes back as he found my G-spot. He knew exactly what he was doing. My thighs shook uncontrollably as he pushed me closer to climax with just a curl of his fingers inside me.

He leaned forward and lightly kissed me on the lips, making my whole body go soft. He really had complete dominance over me. With just his soft touch, he was sending me into spasms of pleasure that I've never felt before.

My hands reached for his arms, feeling his thick biceps as they flexed. He was so powerful. So big.

"You know that nothing was going to stop me until I had you," he said. "I would've hunted you like a man possessed in those school hallways until you gave in to me."

A wave of delight surged through me as he spoke.

"Really? You weren't going to stop?"

"It was my mission. I wanted you from the moment I saw you from the inside of my limo. Scarlett, you are intoxicating."

"I don't usually let boys do this to me, and especially not after just knowing them for a day," I replied. I really didn't want him to think I was a slut, even when he had his fingers deep inside my soaking sex.

Kingsley's other hand found my clit, and I moaned again.

"But I'm no boy, Scarlett," he replied. "I'm a *man*."

"Yes, you most definitely are. No boy can do this to me."

In no time at all, he was bringing me to the very cusp of

climax. I could no longer speak. My head was full of stars and his impeccable smile.

I leaned forward and took his mouth with mine.

And then it was my turn to take control.

I ripped open his jeans like a woman possessed. My hands grasped around his erect member poking out from his underpants as I shuffled down the bed.

"My go," I said. "Let me be your good girl."

Kingsley just groaned and leaned back as my mouth found the wet tip of his throbbing cock.

I took him inside. Sucking on him. Kingsley was a big guy, and his cock was the same. His hands reached down for my hair, guiding my head over his groin. I was full of him.

He groaned. I was clearly doing something right, and I did not stop.

I am loving this. I am loving what I'm able to do to him.

And soon his body was trembling as I felt his cock twitch. I gulped him down. Hot and wet. His groans became unrestricted.

I crawled up the bed so that we were face-to-face. Kingsley wrapped one of his muscular arms around me and pulled me in tight. He kissed me gently on the forehead and whispered a *thank you*.

We lay there in silence for a long time as I contemplated what the hell had just happened.

It was certainly better than any fantasy I'd imagined on that bus home.

* * *

"I'm going to call you Queen from now on," Kingsley announced as he stood in the center of my bedroom, fitting his pants back on.

"What?"

"I'm going to call you Queen, and so now you've really got to call me King. No excuse."

"Ew. Please don't," I replied, pulling a face. "Really. It's so cringe. Please don't."

"Too late," he said with a smile, rushing over to give me a long kiss. "You know, I've never met a girl like you before."

For, like, the third time that evening, I found myself blushing. "Stop being so dramatic, Kingsley. Stop saying things that will make me go all dizzy inside."

"It's true, though."

"Okay, then."

"So, you're going to call me King?"

"I will think about it."

He laughed.

"I've truly never met someone like you, Scarlett."

I gave a mock bow. "Well, thank you."

"And I can't wait to find out more about you."

I better pinch myself. Is this even happening?

I shook my head. "You're crazy. We've only just met and you're saying these things."

"Maybe I am," he said, before heading to the door. "But I am not crazy in knowing that we will smash this scene on Monday, trust me."

"I do," I replied.

Oh, I really do trust him. With all my heart.

And then he was gone.

I fell back onto the bed. The sheets were still warm from where he'd just been. I sighed deeply.

Had I imagined the last few blissful hours? Or was that British boy actually real?

I closed my eyes and stayed in the memory of him.

I couldn't wait for Monday.

8

SCARLETT

It was Monday morning, and I was practically sprinting to get to Crystal River High. All weekend, I had been dreaming of Kingsley.

So many scenarios ran through my mind. Our little performance scheduled for Theater class. Meeting him again.

I had Friday night on repeat in my head like a broken record player, just constantly reveling in his tender but firm touch. The way he made my body shake.

I couldn't wait to see him again.

I got to school and darted through the hallways. As I turned a corner, Liv tried to say hi to me. I replied in passing.

"How was your weekend?" she asked me, wanting to stop for a chat.

"I have so much to tell you," I replied as I skipped past. "So much juicy stuff. But I can't stop now."

I was on a mission. I was looking out for a tall, dark British man. *My* man.

I can't wait to find out more about you.

That's what he said.

But he was nowhere to be found.

His fancy limo wasn't parked out front. There was no sign of him anywhere, but still, I looked around the school hallways. I had to push my way through the crowds of students to make my way through the school, always keeping my eyes on the lookout for the hunk with black hair.

I knew I was being desperate. I knew I didn't want to give my heart so easily to this strange boy with a razor-sharp accent who'd appeared in my life out of nowhere like a tornado. He just sounded too good to be true. Granted, I was *insanely* sexually attracted to him, but what lurked behind those crystal-blue eyes of his? Was he a rogue or a prince? The idea of finding out excited me and made my heart flutter.

I made my way to the rehearsal studio. Maybe he was there, getting ready to perform our scene.

But the only person in the room was Mrs. Stone.

"Hello, Scarlett," she greeted me as I arrived, panting.

"Hi, Mrs. Stone."

"Perfect timing. You're just the person I wanted to see."

"Oh? Me? Why?"

Mrs. Stone stood up from her desk.

"I gave you an assignment to do for today, didn't I? I believe your partner was Kingsley."

"Yes."

"Good news. You don't have to stress about knowing your lines. Lucky for you, it won't be going ahead."

"No?"

"You see, I've just been told that Kingsley's family called in today. He's pulled out of Crystal River High."

The lump in my throat returned. "Pulled out?"

"He's actually leaving back for England," Mrs. Stone replied. "It's actually quite quick. Something must've been wrong. Maybe he didn't like America. Apparently, he's on a flight out today."

I could barely string my words together. My head spun. "Leaving? Today?"

"Yes," Mrs. Stone said, speaking slowly to me like I was not listening. "I've been told he's heading back to London. Such a shame. I really liked his accent."

Without a word, I turned my back on Mrs. Stone and stormed out of the rehearsal room directly for the bathroom. I didn't care what she thought of me. I locked myself in the cubicle.

He's gone.

Back home.

Without telling me?

He really was too good to be true. What a fool I was. Thinking he actually cared about me. I had never felt so young and so *freaking* stupid. My thoughts from the other night now echoed in my head.

You fell for him, Scarlett. He's not going to marry you. Now he's going to give you the worst heartbreak in the world.

And that's when the tears came.

9

ARTICLE FROM RICH & FAMOUS MAGAZINE

There are two eligible billionaire bachelors coming to town, and no one's going to stop them.

Anyone worth anything in London knows the name Heath-Harding. The old aristocratic family stretches back hundreds of years, counting important historic figures such as two Prime Ministers, six Members of Parliament, and one Admiral of the Royal Navy within its descendants. You may even have heard of the current Lord Heath-Harding making loud waves in the London publishing scene in the eighties when he added even more wealth to his already-considerable family fortune by purchasing some very profitable publishing houses in a controversial move that rocked the literary world. A very smart man indeed.

But, while this family may be old, their newest additions are as modern and fresh as they come.

Introducing Kingsley and Duke Heath-Harding, the

current Lord Heath-Harding's two newly adult children with his late wife. These boys have grown up in the luxury that you would expect from such a noble family. But don't let their wealth fool you, they're more grounded than you realize.

Both boys, although born in London, have been raised in the country on their family's ancestral home. A lavish estate. They're both keen sportsmen with whole cabinets full of glittering trophies. Both were such child sports prodigies that they could've either have gone professional at either rugby or football, such were their talents on the field. Educated at the best boarding schools in the country, where they both received top marks, they had the whole world of top-tier universities as their pick.

But now they've both come to London.

And they're both the talk of the town. They're destined for big things. Money. Girls. Parties.

And who can blame them?

They're young. Charming. Smart. Incredibly handsome and muscular. And just downright irresistible to the ladies. They're practically unstoppable.

Certainly, keen aristocratic observers have murmured their approval. "Both Duke and Kingsley are young men with a lot of drive," says one Lord, who's a friend of the family. "They're a hit with women. Both of my daughters, and even my wife, have asked them round for tea. It's taken me a lot of effort to claw my women back."

We've even spoken to an influential Instagram model, a darling of the London fashion scene, who told us how she had met the two Heath-Harding brothers at a private members club in Soho and they absolutely charmed her socks off. "Have you seen their jawlines? My god," she told me, breathless. "It's like the two brothers were made in a lab to be perfect male specimens. I would love to do a photoshoot with the both of them. Imagine being stuck between a Heath-Harding sandwich. Delicious!"

It seems like fame and fortune really does help you in the bedroom. And also, good looks.

And both Duke and Kingsley have those in spades.

A lot is riding on these two boys. Their father is known to be strict and ruthless. There's a lot to be expected from such bright lights.

Can these two dashing bachelors survive being on top of the world in one of the world's top cities? We shall see, but this journalist thinks that they might not only just survive but thrive.

10

FOUR YEARS LATER

SCARLETT

"You're late."

I'm barely through the front door of the restaurant before Clive, my manager, comes bounding over to me with a furious expression on his face. His little beady eyes glower at me before I even get a chance to catch my breath. His thin lips are turned into a sneer, and I find myself braced for his familiar temper.

"Sorry, Clive. I did just call you saying the traffic is terrible and that I might be late," I try to explain. I check the time on my phone. "It's not even ten minutes past my start time. I'll be quick getting changed. I promise. I can work extra late tonight to make up for it."

Clive doesn't even glance down at the time on my phone's screen. Instead, he points a stubby finger aggressively towards my chest. I take a step back in horror. "I don't give a shit about your excuses."

"I did call you..."

"You're on your last warning, Scarlett. Your *last* warning. Don't ever be late again."

He storms off, leaving me sighing by the front door. Clive is a hard man to please, and even harder to work for. I promise myself I won't cry, but it's getting real hard.

Just toughen up and get through this shift, girl. Ignore him.

I head downstairs to change into my work uniform, passing by tables full of families.

London Bridge – my workplace on the main street of Crystal River - is a family restaurant. The whole aesthetic is British-themed in the way that only an American who'd never been to the UK can design it. Lots of pies and chips and gravy with Guinness on the tap and Chinese-made British flags hanging over every part of the wall.

A little bit of London in small town America.

That's the eye-rolling motto written in the sign swaying over the door.

This restaurant is probably further away from London than what you'd get inside a Pizza Hut.

Okay, so my plans for post-high school never did materialize. Things - *life* - got in the way of what I wanted to do past graduation. One thing I failed to factor in with all my time daydreaming about a London life during high school was the teeny tiny fact that dreams actually cost money. Who would've thunk it? You can't board a big jet plane all the way over to the other side of the world when you can't even afford the ticket.

A job that was only meant to be a few months of saving ran up on me and unexpectedly turned into a career. Now I was no longer saving for that dream trip to

London but using the money to pay for bills and rent an apartment. All those things that just deplete your savings account.

Essentially, life happened to me. My London dreams went on pause.

London Bridge is not exactly London itself. Hell, it's not even the next best thing. But it must do for now.

I still live in Crystal River. I work full-time. I still have that black and white poster of Big Ben on the wall. I still dream.

But dreaming is easy, actually *living* the dream is hard.

And there has not been a man in my life since that night with Kingsley. When he disappeared without a word, I realized that it'll take me a lot to trust a man again. No man worth my love. I was a young teenage girl, and I allowed myself to be strung along by some handsome dude with a charming smile. No way was I going to let that happen to me again.

Plus, I'm scared of being rejected like that again. It took a long time for my heart to recover. I can't ever have it exposed like that a second time; I don't know if my heart can possibly take it.

I dump my bag downstairs with the rest of the staff's belongings and get into my work uniform. Tweed jacket and flat cap. Clive likes us waitresses dressed as eighteenth-century chimney sweepers, even if we hate it. Apparently, it's what everyone in London wears. I don't think Clive has even visited the city.

I sigh again and head back up the stairs, ready to start my shift.

I've been doing this job for so long that it's become second nature to me. I dive in between tables like a pro, dealing with messy children and their even-messier parents. I deliver bowls to tables and correct obnoxious customers who call them *fries* even after I've shown them their name on the menu.

"Well, we do it the British way. Over there, they're called *chips*."

It's what Clive wants us to do, to use the slang language straight out of a Dickens book.

Yeah, not exactly the kind of London life I was imagining for myself four years ago. But, hey, it pays the bills.

I smile and nod with enthusiasm. I am good at my job. I'm proud of the work I do. I give families a good day out. What more can you ask?

I pass by Clive a few times on my shift. He just glares at me. That man has something against me, but I don't know what. I try to be friendly towards him, but my attitude doesn't help.

I think he hates me.

"Last chance, Scarlett," he whispers threateningly as he wanders past. Just in case I've forgotten how much of a dick he is.

I really don't know what that man's deal is, but he is my manager. I have to keep him happy, but sometimes I do wish there is a way I can pull that stick from up his ass.

With the other waitresses, we take a London Bridge-themed cake over to an eight-year-old's birthday party and sing happy birthday in exaggerated Cockney accents.

"'Appy Birfday, gu'vena!"

The kid's face lights up as he blows out the candles. Us waitresses clap along. Despite all the crap us waitresses get on this job; I do love seeing happy faces on kids. Clive may be annoying to work for, but there are certainly perks in working here. At least every day there's something different.

The shift gets busier and busier. I'm rushing faster and faster between tables in my section, managing about six different orders and requests at once. I want to earn good tips, and that means staying on top of your serving game.

I get one particularly difficult order from a table, and so I head over to the bar to explain their complicated drinks.

"They want the *London Eye* cocktail without the vodka, the *Trafalgar Square* cocktail without the juice, and the Coke without ice but with a slice of lime."

I spin around to rush back to my section when I collide, head-first, into Clive.

"*Ouch.*"

The man's carrying a drink. Well, he *was* carrying a drink until we made contact. It spills. The contents of the glass go everywhere. All over me. All over him.

We're absolutely soaked in Diet Coke.

And then Clive turns to me, his beady eyes on fire. Soda drips from his nose. It would be a comical sight if I'm not currently absolutely terrified about losing my job.

I know from that expression on his face that I'm in trouble.

I'm already on my last chance and I think I've blown it.

11

SCARLETT

"Oh, god," I say, my hand raising to my shocked mouth. "I'm so sorry, Clive."

My boss just glares at me from behind his wet hair.

"What the *fuck*, Scarlett."

"I'm sorry."

I look down at his shirt. Like me, he is covered in Diet Coke.

"This is your fault," he says angrily. "You ran into me."

Right, he's definitely wrong there. It isn't just my fault, it's Clive's, too. He was moving fast through the restaurant, holding a drink and not keeping a lookout on his surroundings. Something like this was bound to happen. It was, at the very least, an accident. But now he's acting as if I've done it deliberately?

I want to tell him all this, but I've had enough experience of Clive to know he will never listen to me. He never listens to his waitresses. He'll never admit something is his fault.

So, I just grin and bear it.

"I am sorry, Clive. I can go and get you a towel or something."

"No, I'll dry myself off. I'm sure you'll only mess that up as well somehow. This truly is your last warning."

"Okay."

Great.

"Because this is your fault," Clive continues with a sneer. "You will need to make this drink again and apologize to table thirteen. You will need to explain to them that it's *your* fault their drink is late."

I nod towards my tables. "I'm kinda busy right now, Clive. Table thirteen isn't even in my section."

And I'm still wet too, I want to add.

My manager just growls at me. "I don't care. Do it, Scarlett."

I nod and rush away, just happy to get away from him.

I apologize to table thirteen, still covered in Diet Coke, and fetch them a new drink. Then I have to sort out my own tables. I don't even get a moment's chance for myself to dry down for nearly half an hour, and by then I'm smelling of a lovely cocktail of cheap soda and sweat.

The rest of the shift goes equally poorly. We're fully booked, but there's a group of men that arrive demanding a table.

"We don't care that you're full," one of them says. "Find us a table."

Take a deep breath, Scarlett.

"Okay, let me see what I can do for you guys."

I actually manage to squeeze them in. It takes a lot of table gymnastics on the booking system, but it works out.

But the problem is that they end up in my section.

Nice.

It's three guys. All in their thirties. All seemingly rearing for a fight with a stressed-out waitress.

"Right, so I've actually got you a table. I think it all works out. Follow me."

The men only grunt in response. No gratitude. I've worked long enough in hospitality to know not to expect any, though.

They sit and I pass them menus.

"Food here looks shit," the same one who told me to find a table says. The others loudly agree with him.

He's clearly the leader of this pack.

I want to stand there and tell them that if they don't like the food, then they are perfectly free to *just leave*. It is a free country, after all.

But I don't. And they don't.

They order their food. Fine. I jot it down in my notepad and enter it into the till.

A moment later, I find myself walking past their table. Spotting me, they rudely gesture me over with an aggressive wave, like I'm a slave.

"Anything the matter, gentlemen?"

"We want to change our order," Mr. Head Honcho demands.

"That's going to be difficult," I reply. I think of the kitchen already making their food right now and how unhappy they'll be if I told them to scrap it all and start over.

"No, it isn't. You're meant to be our server. The customer is always right. Now, serve us."

Okay. Great.

I take their new order and rush to the kitchen. As expected, I get abuse thrown at me by the Brazilian chef when I tell him to change, mid-making the meal, to something wholly new. I understand his frustration. I just take his yelling in my stride.

And I spot Clive eyeballing me from the bar.

Ignore him, Scarlett.

I continue dashing around *London Bridge*, making sure my section is operating smoothly. The rude guys on the table don't bother me while they wait for food, but I do overhear their conversation as I pass. They're comparing the asses of the waitresses in the restaurant. Scaling them from one to ten. I roll my eyes.

Their food is soon ready, and I bring it over to them. Still no gratitude.

I come back to check on them a few minutes later.

"Everything all good with your food, gentlemen?"

"It's shit."

That's the only response.

"Do you want me to change it, or offer a refund?"

They just completely ignore me and continue munching. I guess the food isn't as shit as they say when they're still eating through it. I stand there awkwardly until I realize they're literally just blanking me before I leave.

I go into the bathroom and take in a deep breath.

I'm usually a strong gal. Calm and collected. I've had a lot of crap thrown at me through life, but today has been especially tough.

It's hard not to cry.

I wipe away the last bits of dried Diet Coke from my hair and step back out into the busy mess of the restaurant.

I scan my eyes over my section.

And then I realize.

The rude men have disappeared.

I run to their table. They're gone, and they haven't paid.

Shit.

That means only one thing.

"Done a runner," I moan under my breath. "The bastards actually did it."

I rush outside the restaurant, hoping to catch them. I should've expected them to run the minute they walked through the doors with that attitude of theirs. I should've kept a sharper eye on them. I should not have let them slip away like that.

Careless, Scarlett.

As soon as I make it past the front doors, a car comes screeching past me and through the parking lot. It nearly hits me on the way out. If I was three feet further ahead, then I would just be a stain on the car's window.

Inside the speeding vehicle are the three men. They have the windows down and are jeering at me. Laughing and mocking. One still has ketchup running from his mouth.

They shoot on out of the restaurant's parking lot, cackling like jackals.

I just stand there, unable to do anything. I'm just in shock at their arrogance and at how stupid I've been to let them get away with that little stunt.

I take a moment before I walk inside.

Yeah, it's getting real hard not to cry right about now.

Once inside the restaurant, Clive is by my side in an instant.

"I saw all that."

"You did?"

"That was your last straw, Scarlett. I can't believe you let them leave."

"What else could I do, Clive?" I can suppress the emotion in my wavering voice. "I couldn't step in front of their car."

"You've failed, Scarlett. Pretty rookie mistake there.

Their tab is coming out of your paycheck, you got that? This was totally our fault."

I turn to look my manager in the eye.

"Screw it. I quit."

"What?"

"I can't take this anymore from you, Clive. I'm out of here. I resign tonight. Right now."

Clive snorts. "And what are you going to do with yourself, Scarlett? You have no university education. You've worked here for years. You're a little failure in life, aren't you? What the hell are you going to even do?"

I look around *London Bridge*. My eyes pass over the tacky fake-British decor. Then I take in a deep breath and stare him down.

"I'm going to do what I should've done years ago. I'm going to London."

12

SCARLETT

"Excuse me," I say loudly as I bend down to face the seating man. He looks up at me in shock. I bet he's wondering why this crazy American girl with a suitcase that's practically the same size as her is actually talking to him. I mean, I have heard Londoners don't like it when strangers talk to them on the Tube, so his expression is pretty justified.

But he does look absolutely terrified.

"Ah, hello. How may I help you?"

Yeah, he's *very* startled.

"Is this the right train to Piccadilly Circus?" I ask. I smile, trying to appear friendly and not crazy. I don't know if it works.

The man nods at me nervously and then quickly goes back to his newspaper.

Honestly, look at me. As if I could be a serial killer on such a busy train. The cliche must be true that Londoners really hate speaking to strangers.

I'm glad that this train goes to Piccadilly Circus, though. I was really worried there for a moment that I might end up on the other side of London than I was aiming for.

I've just got off the plane, hence my massive luggage. I hopped straight onto the next Tube and so here I am. Speeding through the ancient underground system of tunnels below the surface of London. I am here. In this city. On British ground. Well, technically *beneath* it.

Excitement is too tame a word to describe what I'm feeling.

The Tube map is just a maze to my dumb American eyes. I could not get a handle on it when I was in the station, thus forcing me to ask Mr. Startled over here.

A few more stops and the train reaches Piccadilly Circus. I nod a quick *thank you* at the seated man. He ignores the crazy American woman. I pull my heavy suitcase off the Tube and make my way up all the escalators to the ticket hall.

There are just so many people. It makes it so difficult to navigate up the narrow hallways of the Tube station, but I am in total awe. I've not even stepped foot on London's sidewalks yet and I'm bursting with happiness.

I emerge into the daylight like I'm coming out of a cave, and everything is overwhelming. My senses are assaulted.

I'm smack-bang in the middle of Piccadilly Circus, a major roundabout in the West End. Sort of like London's version of Times Square. There are massive, illuminated billboards above me advertising sportswear and soda. There are theater ticket vendors shouting discount prices at passersbys. There are men with carts selling hotdogs. There are crowds of people taking selfies.

I stand there with my bag and spin my head around, taking it all in.

A red double-decker bus zooms past, whipping my hair back.

This. Is. London.

I feel like Hugh Grant or Harry Potter might walk past me. I feel like I'm in a film. I feel like I've been transported into a magical place.

This is certainly not like *London Bridge* in the slightest.

"Wow," I whisper. I want to cry. It's been a lot of time, effort, and money to get me to be standing where I am today. The noise. The traffic. The lights. The people.

This is what I imagined my life to be when I was daydreaming back in Crystal River High, and now I'm here. Right in the heart of things.

Just like I've stepped into a tourist postcard.

I just take an hour to wander around aimlessly. I don't even know what direction I head in; I just want to see it all. I pull along my heavy suitcase and stare up, blinking at all the lights.

Everything just feels so... *new*. Every emotion. I really can't believe I was that spontaneous to just say *screw it* and quit that crappy restaurant job and put all my money into securing a flight over here. I love that I did it, though. I feel in control of my life for once.

The architecture around here is a cool mixture of grand old Victorian style and modern glass. So different from the box-like houses of Crystal River suburbia.

I just carry on walking around, my head twisting and turning at all the sights.

And then it starts to get dark, and I know I must get to my hostel to check-in before it's too late.

I follow the map on my phone. It leads me far away from the bright lights of Piccadilly Circus and the West End and into some dark, curvy streets. It feels a lot different down here. Less touristy. More Jack the Ripper.

Gone are the crowds and smoke; now the only sound is the crunching of my suitcase wheels on the concrete London sidewalks as I trust my phone's maps to find where I'm going.

It makes me turn into a dark alley.

One of London's famous black cabs passes me. The driver leans out the window in my direction.

"You alright, love?" he asks me in a thick London accent.

I lift up my illuminated phone. "I'm fine," I reply.

The taxi speeds off, leaving me alone next to the alleyway.

It would be a shame if I were to get murdered within a few hours of touching down at Heathrow. I can just imagine the headline now in Crystal River's local newspaper.

STUPID GIRL DECIDES TO PACK IT ALL UP AND GO TO LONDON. THEN GETS MURDERED BECAUSE OF SAID STUPIDITY.

I ACTUALLY DON'T GET MURDERED. INSTEAD, I reach the end of the dark alley and have somehow made it to my final destination.

My hostel.

The outside looks like it hasn't been cleaned or painted since Charles Dickens walked these streets. Inside is no better. There's a leak down one wall. Chairs that probably haven't been moved since the seventies.

Sure, it's not the swankiest of hotels on offer in London, but it's cheap. And it's a bed. I'll take that over a park bench.

I need to be serious about it. Pretty soon I will be

running out of savings, so a park bench might seriously be on the agenda in a few weeks.

This is all I can afford until I get a much-needed job.

Everything rides on the next few days. Get a job. Get a flat. Try to survive in this big, bad city.

But I'm excited for the adventure to come.

I check-in. The hostel receptionist is a girl in her late twenties. There's no one else in the foyer; I guess it's late. Or, more likely, there are no other guests crazy enough to stay here.

The hotel receptionist immediately picks up my accent when I speak to her.

"You're American?" she asks.

"Don't hold it against me."

Her eyes widen. "Oh my god, I absolutely adore New York City."

"I've never been," I reply. "It's pretty far from me, actually. Small town America, that's me."

The receptionist gestured around the shambles of a room. "Why did you bother coming here?"

"Well, it's always been my dream to live in London," I explain with a shrug. "Things back home got a bit too much, so I decided to sell nearly everything I own and make the journey over the Pond."

She shakes her head at me. "You sound insane. Good luck to you. Welcome to the biggest shithole on earth."

Yeah, I probably am insane.

She hands me my room key. This must be the last place in London to use actual physical keys for rooms instead of electronic cards, and I don't think it was some cool retro aesthetic choice.

I tighten my fingers around the handle of my suitcase and drag it towards the hallway. As I reach the door, the receptionist calls out.

"I know what you need to do, don't you?"

"What's that?"

"You need to find yourself a nice British man."

"Um... sure. Thanks for the advice."

The receptionist nods at me like she's an old sage, imparting indispensable wisdom. I just continue on my way.

But the very last thing on my mind is a man. Trust me. Ain't doing that again anytime soon.

I head upstairs to my room. Each step creaks ominously as I pull up my suitcase. I'm terrified that I could fall through the staircase at any moment.

I shut the door to my room and make sure it's locked. The room contains literally just a single bed pushed up against the wall. There's not enough space to swing my arms about. There's only one shower on this floor, and it's communal.

I'm really not complaining though, at least this means I can only go upwards from here.

I sit down on the squeaky bed and suddenly feel super tired. All the excitement of the day hits me at once. I lie down and think of the checklist I need to start.

Job and flat and don't get involved with a British man.

They are what I need to get sorted as soon as possible.

Outside my window, I can hear shouting. I shut my eyes to the lovely sounds of a drug deal going wrong. Lots of yelling in rough British accents. Very idyllic.

I can't believe it.

I really am in London.

"Just like Dorothy," I whisper to myself. "I guess I'm not in Kansas anymore."

13

SCARLETT

FINDING a job in this city is a lot harder than I initially thought.

I'm walking down a street just off Piccadilly Circus. Shaftesbury Avenue. It's morning, and there's sunshine. Which surprises me as I had expected London to have nothing but drizzling rain - that's the cliche, isn't it - but today is actually very pretty.

This is the center of the theater district. There are rows of old theaters here. Buildings as old as America. I still can't believe all the history that's happened on these streets. The history that's treated so casually by the British. To my fresh American eyes, I'm just dumbfounded.

I head into the nearest theater and go straight to the box office.

"Hello, I'm looking for a job and would love to apply here. I've got my CV with me."

The man behind the desk regards me with a nonchalant frown.

"We're not accepting any job applications at present."

"Oh, okay. Thank you."

I try to keep upbeat. The man doesn't.

I head on out of there and walk into the next theater along.

Same deal.

"I've got my CV if you'll like."

"We're not looking for anyone."

"Right. But I can still give it to you if you need staff. It's got my phone number and email on there."

"I'm not taking your CV."

"Okay. Have a good day."

Outside, I take in a deep breath and try to think positively. It's hard.

Two rejections in just as many minutes? Yeah, finding a job in this city is pretty damn difficult.

Variants of that interaction happen at every theater I go to. No one wants to interview me, let alone even just read my CV. Each theater is another stab in my heart. Each rejection is another twist of the dagger into my dreams.

Needing a break, I grab a sandwich from a shop and head into Hyde Park, one of London's biggest Royal Parks. I sit on a bench by the lake and stare despondently at the ducks.

"I thought things would be easier than this," I say to a passing swan as I bite into my prawn sandwich. "I thought I could get a job working in a theater seeing plays every night. That would've been really cool, but I guess it's not meant to be."

It's good to rest my legs. I've been walking all day.

Maybe this whole dream was a stupid idea. Maybe I'm not cut out for London. It seems like everything is against me staying.

Why did I spend all my money coming here? Have I just been a big old idiot?

Maybe coming here was a mistake if I can't even find a lowly theater job.

I shake my head. Negativity is going to get me nowhere. I flip out my phone and check my emails. There's one about a possible flat viewing in an hour. I've been applying for rental accommodation as well as jobs today.

Maybe going to check out this place might get me in a better mood.

I throw my sandwich wrapper in the nearest bin and head for the nearest Tube station.

* * *

IF I'D THOUGHT that the flat viewing would go any different to my job applications, then I was severely wrong.

"So, you're American?" the estate agent asks me as I looked around the tiny bedsit. The entire flat is a converted attic. If you lay down in the bed, then your face would be mere inches away from the kitchen sink. You have to navigate around the toilet just to get out in the morning. There's practically no space for either the estate agent or me to stand in the room together unless we want to get intimate.

"Yep, I flew in yesterday," I reply.

"So, I'm assuming you've got no rental history in the UK?"

I shake my head. "Nope. I literally got off the plane this time yesterday."

"Hm," the estate agent narrows her eyes at me. "Then this is going to be extremely difficult."

"Oh, I can offer you the deposit straight away, and I've got enough money saved for a few months of rent," I protest.

The estate agent doesn't budge. "Miss Hart, I don't

think you realize how difficult renting a flat in this city without any rental history in this country is going to be for you."

Oh no.

I sigh. "Please, just give me a chance, okay? I need somewhere to live. I'm a good tenant, I promise."

"I can't give you a flat based on your character," the estate agent replies firmly. "Or a promise. You need documentation. Forms. Rental history."

"I can give you the email of my landlord in the US."

"No can do."

"Oh, okay."

And that's it. Flat viewing over.

Somehow it had gone even worse than my job applications.

I step out into the street. The sunshine of the morning has given way to ominous black clouds and a sprinkling of rain. *Now* it's the London weather cliche.

Perfect. Even the weather is rejecting me.

The estate agent gets into her car and drives away. I'm back to being alone.

I look back up at the flat that won't be mine. I look at the sign for the nearest Tube station.

It's time to take matters into my own hands.

I rush onto the next train bound for central London and I go back to Shaftesbury Avenue. I march into the closest theater and head straight to the box office. The sign above the building reads *The Prestige Theater*.

"I would like to see the theater manager," I command the assistant when I step up to the box office.

"What's this for?"

"A job interview."

"Give me one minute."

She thinks I'm here for a pre-booked interview. Well,

I'm not going to discourage her. The assistant makes a phone call while I stand there, hair wet from the rain, and wait.

I resolve not to leave this old building until I've got an interview.

Soon, a man dressed in a suit appears at the bottom of the staircase. He's got a clipboard in his hand. He strolls over to me.

"I'm Giles," he says. "The theater manager. You're here for an interview?"

"Yes," I reply. I raise my chin to act confidently. "I'm Scarlett."

The man checks his clipboard.

"I don't have your name written down here," he says.

Well, there's no point lying. "That's because I've just rocked up. I'm looking for a job. I have my CV here and I can start immediately."

Giles shakes his head in exactly the same way the estate agent did. My heart drops. "I'm sorry, but I've got a tight schedule today. I can't interview anyone who hasn't already applied."

I thrust my hand into my bag and pull out a copy of my CV. "Well, please take this. I'm serious about working. I can really start straight away."

"I'm sorry, Scarlett."

"Just take the CV," I say, practically pleading with the man. "If you need anyone at all, then you have this. I'm only a phone call away. I need a job, Giles."

The man frowns. He's bald with pale lips. His hands have the yellow skin of a serial smoker. He's probably in his mid-thirties, but he looks older.

"Fine then."

He takes my crumbled CV and attaches it to his clipboard.

"So, can I have an interview?" I ask.

Giles shakes his head again. "I'm sorry, Scarlett, but I have to stick to my schedule. Good day."

He turns and heads back up the staircase.

I wander out of the theater, completely and utterly dejected.

14

SCARLETT

WELL, that's it then. I guess my London dream is truly over. Even I, with my upbeat attitude, can only endure a certain number of rejections in a day before I decide to call it quits.

I was so silly to think I could just fly over here and make a life for myself. I should've listened to everyone back home who warned me, but I was way too strong-headed to take heed when I boarded that plane.

And now I've ended up penniless wandering the streets of London in the rain.

I can imagine the headline for the local Crystal River newspaper.

STUPID GIRL FOLLOWS STUPID DREAMS. FAILS.

. . .

I snort at my dark joke. Well, at least all this is a story to tell the grandkids.

I pass by a row of shops. I check myself out in the window's reflection. My hair is wet from the rain, but I don't care anymore. It's not like this day can get any worse.

There's a whole bunch of notices in the window. Little handwritten and printed notes. People trying to sell old furniture. Escorts and drug dealers offering up their services. I scan over them, curious. And then I come across one different from the rest.

VACANCY.

NEED A FLATMATE ASAP. LOOKING FOR YOUNG WOMAN TO SHARE WITH YOUNG WOMAN. NO MEN. REALLY. MEN, DON'T CALL ME.

I laugh at the note and turn to start walking away.

But...

You know what? Screw it. I might as well try this. If I get murdered in some bedsit, then that's the risk I'm going to have to take to find a place to sleep in this city. And I do like how insistent she is about her *no men* policy.

I turn back to the notice and immediately call the phone number.

A hurried voice answers. She's female, so that's a good sign. At least it's not some middle-aged creepy man wanting me to be his "personal companion".

"Hi?"

"Hello, I've just walked past your sign in the window for the flatmate vacancy. I'm talking to the right person about that, right?"

There's a short pause before she speaks again, this time full of bubbling energy. "Oh. Right. Hello! No one's called up about that. This is strange."

"Wow. Well, I'm looking for somewhere to live."

"You're female?"

"Hopefully I sound it."

"Are you free now?" she asks me.

"Now?"

"Yeah, can you come over right now?"

"Uh, yeah. Sure."

"Great, come over."

The girl quickly gives me an address. I commit it to memory.

"I'm heading there now," I say.

"Fantastic. I'll be waiting."

Then she hangs up.

I smile. My god, I might've actually found a place.

Calm down, Scarlett. You need to actually meet this girl first. She could be nuts. Even more nuts than you.

But still, my excitement can't hide away. My phone's map says the flat isn't too far away. I start to skip towards it.

* * *

I'm walking through the park that's opposite the address when I see the commotion.

Loud noises.

Shouting.

I look to see what's going on. According to my phone's map, I should be practically standing on top of the flat I'm here to see.

The commotion is coming from a place above a fish and chip shop. There's a girl, dressed only in a dressing gown, throwing cardboard boxes out of a window onto the street and shouting. Another girl is standing in the middle of the street, surrounded by a debris of clothes and books, yelling back at the girl in the window above. A proper yelling match is going on between the two.

"Why are you being so crazy?" The girl on the street cries out.

Window girl's face turns into a snarl. She wraps her dressing gown around her body tighter and yells back equally loud. "Me? Crazy?"

"Yeah, I'm talking about you!"

"I am *not* crazy. You're the one who hasn't paid rent in two months. Crazy, my arse. Also, you brought over two guys last night. You kept me up all night with your insanely loud bonking."

"Well, *whoop-de-doo*, I have had *sex*. I had more of it last night than you've had in three bloody years."

"The whole of London could hear you shagging!"

"Oh, yeah?"

"And, worse of all, you haven't taken the bins out for *three bloody weeks*."

"You really are crazy, Grace!"

"Get out of here," Grace in the dressing gown yells back before she throws another cardboard box down at the girl in the street. "Take your massive collection of dildos. I don't want them."

The cardboard box smashes on the ground, revealing its contents. Just like Grace had screamed, it's a box full of differently shaped sex toys.

I want to laugh, but I stay silent. I don't want to attract any yelling my way.

"Oh my god, Grace. Throwing my shit all over the street? Really? I don't even want any of this stuff. You. Are. Mental."

"Then get outta here."

"Oh, don't worry, Grace. Already way ahead of you."

The girl on the street scoffs and swears before she throws up a middle finger at Grace. The window girl blows a raspberry back.

The dildo girl harrumphs and marches past me.

"She is crazy," she tells me as she passes. "Never live with someone like that."

She rounds the corner and disappears, leaving all her stuff out on the street around me. Everyone in the surrounding buildings and flats has come out to watch.

I check my phone. Grace's flat above the fish and chips shop is my destination.

Oh.

I guess Grace was the girl who put up the vacancy sign. I guess she's the girl I spoke to on the phone.

I gulp.

Grace is still in the window. She's shaking her head in anger. Her dressing gown threatens to unravel.

"Uh, hello," I shout towards her.

She shoots me a look full of daggers. "Hello?"

"I think we just talked on the phone," I say, hesitant. "About the flat vacancy."

Grace frowns at me for a moment, and then she bursts out in a big, charming smile. "Oh, hello! Lovely to see you. Forget about the mess or the crazy former flatmate."

She acts like it's nothing, but it'll be pretty hard to forget about the absolute bombsite of panties and dildos that cover the street.

"Is now really a good time?" I ask, having to raise my voice to reach her in the window. I glance nervously around at all the spectators hanging on to our every word. "I can always come back later."

Grace waves her hand dismissively. "No, now is a perfect time. Give me a minute to get ready."

"Um... Take all the time you need."

"I'm *so* hungry. Let's get some food."

She suggests it casually, like we're best friends and not that I've just witnessed her totally losing her shit in public.

"Sounds good."

I want to get away from everyone watching; if that means food, then I'm all for it.

Grace points a finger at me. "Wait there. I'll come down."

"Sure."

I glance around again at all the previous flatmate's belongings littering the street. Grace really chucked all these out the window? Because her previous flatmate had loud sex and didn't put the bins out for a few weeks?

I don't know whether to stay and meet the girl or contact the nearest mental asylum.

15

SCARLETT

WHEN GRACE SAID she was hungry, I thought she meant she was going to get food from somewhere far away from where she threw her former flatmate's crap all over the street. But, instead, she appears at her flat's doorway and gestures me into the fish and chip shop right under her place.

Oh. We're having food here, then.

"Come on," she says. "Let's go here."

She steps over a dildo to go inside. She's still wrapped up in only a dressing gown.

I nervously glance around at all the locals watching the commotion. This has certainly been a crazy few minutes, and I have a feeling it's going to get even crazier.

Screw it.

I follow her inside the fish and chip shop.

"Hello Rick," Grace greets the shop owner, a big man wearing a greasy apron behind the counter. He's wrapping up a big, battered fish in paper.

When he sees her, a big smile spreads across the man's face and he speaks to her in an accent I cannot understand. He's pure Cockney, through and through. It's like he's trying to talk through a mouthful of marbles.

"'Ere dahlin', wots all dat business outside?"

"Oh, that was my old flatmate. Absolute cow. I'll clean it up later."

Rick winks at her. "Nah worries, luv. What ya havin'?"

"I'll have the usual," Grace says. She turns to me. "You hungry?"

I nod. "Yeah, a tiny bit. I'm not starving for a big meal or anything. I can just have a few chips."

"She'll have the same as me," Grace tells the shop owner before skipping over to a table and sitting. "This is the best chippy in London, hands down. You'll love it here. Rick is great, and he treats me like a princess."

"Great," I reply, sitting down opposite her.

Grace leans forward, her light blue eyes glittering at me. She has long, black wavy hair and pale skin. Her accent is softer than a lot of Londoners I've met, but she's definitely from here. She's like a whirlwind of charming personality, and I'm still suffering from whiplash from being too close. It's like she hasn't stopped moving since she threw those dildos out the window.

She is just so pretty. I'm so envious of her lovely, full, red lips. She's feisty, and I love that.

"Oh, god. Where are my manners?" she says, offering out her hand. "Sorry. I'm Grace Madden."

"Scarlett Hart." I shake her hand.

Her eyes widen at my voice. "You're American?"

"Yep."

"Cool. I've always wanted to go there."

I gesture to the front door behind me. "Outside just then looked pretty intense. You okay?"

She rolls her eyes and groans. "Yep. Sorry you had to see all that. She was not cool. But you know what? I'm glad she's gone."

"What happened?"

"Oh, she slept with half of London at the same time. I don't care about that kind of stuff, but it's the fact that she kept me up all night that really pissed me off. And she didn't pay rent for the last few months. I'm not a homeless shelter. I've been meaning for her to go for the last few weeks, hence the vacancy notice in the shop window. I just didn't expect anyone to call other than some creepy dude."

I laugh. "Well, hopefully, I'm not as bad as a creepy dude."

She glances me up and down. "You most certainly are not. Why did you call me, of all people? Even I can admit that vacancy notice in some shop's window was not the best advertisement."

"I just saw the thing and thought, why not give it a try?"

Grace smiles. "That's so cool and impulsive. I like it. I like you."

That makes me blush.

"Stop it."

"No," Grace continues, taking hold of my hand tenderly. "You are so pretty and *so* American. I love that. I think we're going to get along."

"So, is your flat directly above this chippy?" I ask her, trying quickly to change the subject.

Grace laughs loudly. "Oh, yes. Rick is so kind that he never complains about my stomping around. And, trust me, I love to dance. Isn't that right, Rick?"

The man is strolling over with two massive plates of fish and chips.

"Wot?" he asks.

"I'm just telling my new friend, Scarlett, that you put up with my nuisance."

Rick smiles and dumps the plates in front of us with a hearty chuckle. "You know I luv ya, princess."

I gawk at the size of the steaming pile of salty chips and battered cod presented before me.

"How much do I owe you?" I ask the man.

He waves his hand. "On da 'ouse," he says. "Grace knows she can eat 'ere for free anytime. A friend of Grace is a friend of mine."

"Wow. Thank you."

Grace winks at me. "See? Best chippy in all of London. And Rick's such a sweetheart. He's always looking out for me. When I come home late and drunk, he always asks if I'm alright."

"He sounds lovely."

We both start to eat. The fatty fries and fish are exactly what I need after the stress of today. It's so yummy.

I think I really like Grace. She really did seem crazy at first, but I just love her authentic eccentricity. I can see there's also a kindness to her. After a day of embarrassing rejection and struggle, it's nice to meet someone who's just genuinely friendly. It's renewing my faith in this city.

"Right, let's talk business," Grace says. "This flat. Let me tell you about it."

"Please do."

"I'm technically the landlord. It used to be my mum's and now it's mine, so I run it. I prefer to not go through estate agents if I can. I've had a few bad experiences with them already. As you can probably tell, I need someone to come in and take over the spare room immediately. Just pay me every month and not have super loud threesomes every night and you'll be better than any housemate I've had for years."

I shrug. "Well, I'm looking for a place to move in as soon as possible, and threesomes are very much off the menu for me."

Grace leans back in her seat and wipes her hands on a napkin. "Oh, perfect. Obviously, you can have a look around before you commit, but I'm sure you'll like it."

"I'd love to have a look if that's okay."

"Fantastic." She lowers her voice into a whisper. "I do have to tell you about something important, though."

"What?"

"There is a fox clan living next to the bins. I've tried to shoo them away, but they keep coming back. I think they really like my leftover curry, which is funny because even I don't like it."

I chuckle. "A fox clan doesn't scare me."

"Ah, you're a *tough* American."

"Sure am."

"How long have you been living here?"

"I literally got off the plane yesterday?"

Grace's eyes widen at my comment. "Yesterday? As in the day before today? What have you been up to?"

"Just job hunting and not much else, I'm sad to report."

"Nothing else?"

"Not really."

"You haven't gone around town? Done the tourist things?"

I shake my head. "Haven't had the chance to."

Grace leaps up from her chair and offers a helping hand to me. "My God, what terrible news. I've been such a bad host."

"What do you mean?" I ask her.

Grace pulls me up from the table. "Come on, I'm taking you on a tour of the city. I'm going to welcome you to London. Properly."

16

SCARLETT

After saying goodbye to Rick, Grace leads me down the street towards the nearest Tube station and that's when I start to smile.

"I think we're gonna be good friends," she tells me as we board the next train heading into the West End.

"I think so too."

With Grace holding my hand and talking excitedly, I feel like things are finally starting to get better. My day is no longer a crapshow.

"I can't wait to introduce you to this city," she says.

"Me too."

"I'm going to show you the side of London that tourists don't see. I actually feel pretty honored to be the first person to give you a look around."

"Well, now I'm *very* excited, Grace."

We get off at the Leicester Square Tube station and Grace proceeds to give me a whirlwind tour of the city. It's wild, just like her personality. She practically pulls me by the hand along busy London streets, keen to show me every-thing. She was not kidding when she said she wanted to give me a tour of the city that's beyond anything touristy. She especially loves to point out places that mean some-thing personal to her.

Soon we're off the busy roads around Piccadilly Circus and we dart into the narrow streets of Soho.

"I went on a really bad date there," she tells me, pointing at a bar decked out in rainbow flags. "He just wanted to snog me the minute we sat down at our table. He didn't even want to talk!"

"That sounds horrible."

"Oh, no. It was lots of fun. I had to push him off me. He was *not* happy about that, let me tell you. The bouncers kicked him out of the place and now I'm friends with the two of them. Hello Larry and Gary!"

She waves at the two massive bouncers standing outside the bar. They nod back.

"They're called Larry and Gary," she tells me. "How cute."

We wander down Old Compton Street, the main thor-oughfare of Soho. There are gay nightclubs and trendy bars and little eateries. The nightlife center of the West End.

And it seems like Grace has been on a date or has got blind drunk at every single place along the street.

"And that's where I had an actual good date," she says, pointing at a French bar. "He was pretty charming. But then, two more dates later, he turned out to be incredibly boring and even more rude. So that whole thing faded away pretty damn quickly. Prince Charming, he was not."

She tells me she grew up in London. Moving all around the city until her mum bought the flat she lives in now when she was still a girl. She loves the city. She tells me she'll never move out of it, no matter how expensive it gets.

"And London gets even more expensive every year," she says. "But follow me. I know all the tricks on how to live on a budget in this godforsaken city."

I love Grace's carefree attitude to life. Her spark. It is so infectious. I laugh and giggle along with her like two naughty schoolgirls on a day trip.

This tour has definitely turned into more of a journey through Grace's dating history more than a guide to all the sights, but I'm not complaining. She tells me about long summer nights spent dancing in nightclubs. Drinking till sunrise. Meeting people from all over the world in every walk of life in the smoking areas of seedy pubs. It all sounds so different from my small town back home.

With every story, I feel more at home here. Grace's life is the London life I've been dreaming about. I think I don't even need to check her flat. I feel like I've found someone I connect with on such a deep level.

She takes me deep into Mayfair, a posh side of London with tall white buildings and expensive hotels.

"That's the Palace nightclub," she says, pointing out a closed door on the other side of the road. "I guess it isn't time for them to open just yet. That's one of the most exclusive clubs in this town. It's basically impossible to get into that place unless you're, like, ridiculously wealthy or a movie star. I've tried to weasel my way inside nearly half a dozen times over the past couple of years, but was always unsuccessful. My advice is to simply don't even bother attempting to get in."

"Oh, okay."

"There are better places to go," she says. "Cheaper and less snobby places. Let me take you there."

She pulls me into a tiny little bar. She waves at the bartender and he brings over a bottle of wine for us to share. He grins at Grace.

"That's Tom," she tells me after he heads down to the other side of the bar. "I've known him for years. Gay as anything. He can get you into any club in London. He can talk his way through any bouncer or VIP event. Trust me, I've seen him do it."

I chuckle and drink my wine.

"I am *loving* this tour, Grace. You seem to really know the place."

"I'm glad you do, and of course I know the place. It's where I live."

"London is the polar opposite of home for me, but thanks to you, I think I'm going to enjoy it immensely."

We empty the rest of the wine bottle into our glasses.

"So," she says. "Scarlett, I feel like I've just been telling you everything about myself for hours. Now it's your turn."

"Well, as you know, I'm American. Home is a place called Crystal River."

Grace shakes her head, disappointed in my answer. "Come on, Scarlett. I don't want to know about your Wikipedia page," she says. "I want stories. The proper juicy ones. Tell me, have you been on any bad dates?"

I blush. "Scarlett, it's clear from today that my life is nowhere near as fun as yours."

"Nonsense. There must be something."

"Well, there was one guy." I decide to tell her. She seems like someone who'll understand. "He was British, actually. From London. He came to spend a semester at my high school, but he only lasted a week before he ran back home like a coward..."

I recount the story of Kingsley to Grace. She listens raptly to my tale of heartbreak and love. She barely touches her wine as I breeze through my pain.

"Wow, that's some serious shit," she says when I finish.

"He was my only love. But then he left. It took me a long time to get over him."

"Imagine if you ran into him again," Grace whispers conspiratorially. "In *London*."

I scoff. "As if."

"Well, you are in the same country. Hell, the same bloody city. Crazier things have happened."

"I would never want to see that man again," I reply. "Never."

"And what if you did? What if he walked past us in this bar *right now*?"

I chuckle darkly. "I would probably kill him."

Grace squeals. "Damn, I love that energy. I'll be in the jail cell right alongside you, sister."

"And what about you? I know you've been a serial dater, but has there ever been a man good enough to snare Grace Madden's heart?"

She scoffs and takes a sip of wine. "Well, if you must know... There was a man. Once. It was deep and passionate. And, like you, that also ended in heartbreak."

I mockingly raise my glass. "Cheers to us both having our hearts broken, but still here to tell the tale."

There's a long pause as Grace stares at me. It's like she's evaluating me.

Eventually, she speaks.

"You know, I think I really like you," she says. "I've made my final judgment. You're free to have the room, Scarlett Hart, if you'll have it."

I don't even have to think about it before I answer back.

"I mean, I haven't even seen it yet, but I'll definitely take it."

17

SCARLETT

"WOULD YOU LIKE A CUP OF TEA?" Grace asks me from the kitchen.

"No, thank you," I call back. "I'm fine."

I cross my legs and lean back against Grace's soft sofa. We're back from our tour of the West End and now are relaxing in her flat.

Grace returns to the living room holding a cup of tea close to her chest. She sits down next to me and takes a long gulp of it. She winks at me, and I wink back.

Her flat is small but cozy. It's a two-bedroom place sharing a single bathroom. A kitchen and a living room that's just big enough for the two of us. Not bad for somewhere so close to central London.

Grace has already shown me around. A few paper drawings are hanging on the kitchen wall – she says they're *original compositions* of baby Grace's – and photos of her and her mom scattered around the living room. Her mom looks just like her, so beautiful and smiley. They look happy together.

With our own bedrooms and shared living room and with no one else living with us, Grace tells me it's practically impossible to rent a place like this in London for the price she's willing to offer me. I believe her.

"So, you own this place?" I ask her. "Is that what you said?"

Grace nods. "Yeah, mom bought it years ago for super cheap."

"Oh, cool," I reply. "And where's your mom now?"

Grace shuffles forward and puts the tea down on the table. "She passed away a few years ago."

Oh.

My heart breaks for her. "I'm sorry to hear that."

"Thank you," she replies. "She passed away just as I was turning into an adult. Poor timing on her end, but that was what she was like. Never on time."

"I'm sorry I asked you about her. I shouldn't have said anything," I say quietly. *Damn*, I feel awkward. I should've guessed something was wrong, especially with all the old photos of the two in the living room and no recent ones. Why do I always get myself into uncomfortable conversations like this? "I'm such a doofus."

"It's perfectly fine," Grace replies. "She passed the house onto me, and I've lived here ever since. I'm super lucky not to have to worry about my living situation in London now. It was like a parting gift from her in some strange way."

"What was she like?" I ask. "Your mom?"

"Oh, beautiful," Grace replies, smiling at the memory. "She was *so* beautiful. We got on so well, more like best friends than mom and daughter. She raised me in this city as a single mother with little pay. She was so bloody tough, surviving London with a demanding young girl. I took her for granted until she was gone, and now I miss her every single day."

"I bet."

"She had the most infectious laugh. Nothing could grind her down, not even having me screaming and being an annoying little troublemaker all day."

"She sounds like an amazing woman."

"She truly was. You know, she said the best thing she ever did in her life was a backpacking trip around Europe when she was twenty-two, the same age as I am now."

"No way."

"She loved that experience. She always spoke to me about it, and I loved to listen to her. I loved how happy she was talking about it. She said her favorite part of the trip was when she visited the Sistine Chapel in Rome. She said that Michelangelo's painting on the roof there was the most beautiful thing she's ever seen. Well, until I came along, of course. Ever since she told me about the art on the ceiling, I've wanted to go and visit it."

"I can imagine you would."

"Especially now that I'm the same age as her when she went," Grace continues. "I've been saving to go for ages, but it's been hard. I want to see the Sistine Chapel for myself. I think it'll bring me closer to her, even though she's gone. Do you know what I mean, or am I just sounding mad?"

I nod. "Yeah, I think I do."

Grace makes herself comfy on the sofa. "You sure you don't want a cup of tea?" she asks me.

I smile at her. "I'm sure."

"Okay, but now you're sounding like the mad one."

I nod towards the TV sitting in the corner. "What do you like to watch on there, then?"

Grace practically leaps up in excitement. "Oh my god, I

am the biggest *true crime* junkie in the world," she tells me breathlessly. "I have to tell you about it. I watch hours of documentaries about serial killers and murderers every day. Can't get enough. I'm addicted. Do you watch true crime?"

I shrug. "I've seen a few documentaries."

Grace giggles, delighted, like I'm going to be a new project of hers. "Oh, I'm going to get you *hooked*."

I laugh. "So, you're a big fan of people who kill other people? Maybe I shouldn't have agreed to renting this place..."

Grace shakes her head. "A big fan of people who kill other people? Like you wouldn't believe. I know it's pretty twisted, but I actually listen to true crime podcasts in the gym. When people there are hyping themselves up with hip hop, I'm hyping myself up with a detailed description of how some girl was hacked to pieces in a forest."

"That's disgusting."

Grace nods. "I am so weird. You know, I was once hired at the Sherlock Holmes Museum on Baker Street. I didn't even last a week there. I was fired because *apparently,* I knew too much about Victorian crimes and for correcting customers and the other staff too many times. They didn't want me there at all. They called me difficult. I want to get a tea mug with that written on it. *Difficult.*"

I snort in laughter. "I think your previous flatmate was right. You *are* crazy."

Grace playfully taps me on the arm. "Shut up," she giggles. "Are you absolutely *sure* you don't want a cup of tea?"

"For the hundredth time, Grace. I'm fine."

She narrows her eyes at me. "Do you even drink tea?"

"I'm American," I explain. "I prefer coffee."

She gasps. "That's treasonous in this country. We might

have to do a repeat of the War of Independence here. Have our own London version of the Boston Tea Party."

For the dozenth time that afternoon, I'm laughing again. I haven't done this much laughing for years. I love Grace. She really knows how to make me feel joy. I've been missing that in my life for a long time; I've been too busy working long shifts and trying to save money to even just have a good time sitting down and having a right laugh with someone.

I think our living situation is going to go super well.

My phone buzzes in my pocket. I nearly jump up in shock. I just got my new UK number yesterday, so I'm not expecting any phone calls.

The number is not listed, but I still answer. Grace takes another sip of tea, curious.

"Hello?"

"Is this Scarlett Hart?"

It's a man's voice.

"Speaking."

"It's Giles Bonner here, the theater manager at the Prestige Theater. I believe you came in yesterday and we spoke briefly?"

"Right. Hello!"

It's the man who rejected my job application. Grace throws me a look, curious.

"I know it's very short notice, but we're actually down a lot of staff tonight for the big press night of our latest show. Would you mind coming in? We'll pay you."

I take in a deep breath.

"Is this going to a permanent position, then?" I ask.

There's a short pause on the other end.

"Yes, if you'll like to join our team."

"I will, thank you."

"Okay. I'll send you through the details for tonight's press show to your email address."

"Thank you."

"Welcome to the Prestige Theater."

After Giles hangs up, I spring out of the sofa and do a little happy dance in the middle of the living room. Grace admires me with a smile.

"What was that about?" she asks.

"I just got a job," I reply. "At my dream place. A theater. And I'm starting tonight."

18

SCARLETT

I MEET Giles at the stage door.

"Follow me," he says, ushering me inside the theater.

"Thank you so much for the opportunity," I tell him as we pass the stage door. This must be where all the actors come and sign in before each performance. I feel like I'm being taken into a secret world.

"Press night is going to be one of our busiest nights of the year," he says over his shoulder. "Be alert and don't screw up."

"Sure will."

"Tonight is a very stressful night for us, as you can imagine."

"I bet it is."

He guides me backstage. He acts like it is super casual to just wander through the tight hallways of an ancient theater, but I am floored by amazement and awe at the sheer *awesomeness* of the place. There are old posters of shows from a hundred years ago hanging on the walls.

Signatures of actors long dead. Dressing rooms with costumes hanging over the doors. It is a whole lot of theatrical history all in one place.

This is what I came to London to see.

I imagine what I would've made of all this as the little girl passionately reading books about theater back on the bus to school. I can't believe I'm actually here, in London. In an *actual* theater.

We arrive at the front of house staffroom. There's a whole load of ushers getting changed into their work uniform. Ties and suits and badges. Overwhelming chaos as everyone talks to each other and people rush in and out of the room. Giles had asked for my sizes in the email he sent me, and now he quickly thrusts a bag containing a uniform into my hands.

"Go and get changed," he says. "Here's India. She'll look after you tonight. Make sure you follow what she says at all times."

He calls over a girl around the same age as me. She's tall, with frizzy hair and dark eyes. She nods at me.

I get changed into the work uniform. I'm just so excited to be here and I feel incredibly nervous. Everyone in the staffroom talks about press night in hushed tones. I guess it really is a big deal here. Apparently, there are going to be lots of journalists coming in to review it. Lots of celebrities as well coming to see the show. It really is the most important night of a play's run.

"I don't even know what's playing," I tell India. "What is the show?"

She frowns. "It's a new play."

"Right."

"You finished?" she asks me, looking disapprovingly at my awful attempt at tying up a tie.

She's very dry. Very English. She's as sour as Grace is

eccentric. I decide to give her a dazzling smile. I'll wear her down with my American cheeriness.

"Yep. All good."

"Follow me."

And, once again, I find myself passing through the narrow hallways of the theater. We head downstairs into the auditorium.

"Do you like working here?" I ask India, trying to be friendly.

"It's a job," she replies bluntly. Nothing else.

Wow. She's like a stone wall.

"I'm really excited to work here," I say. "I love theater. Do you like theater?"

"Great." That's her only curt reply. She takes me to a corner and points to the ground. "This is where you are tonight. You watch the show and make sure no one in the audience is on their phone, alright? You take people to the bathroom and make sure they don't cause too much of a disturbance during the show."

"Got you."

India points to a curtain covering a door next to us. "Do not let anyone go out that exit during the show. It creates a lot of noise and only leads outside, even though they might think it leads to the bathroom."

"Gotcha."

"If there is one thing you do tonight," she continues. "Above everything else, do *not* let anyone out that exit, okay?"

"Yep."

"Here," she picks up a stack of programmes. There are not many pages to each one. "Sell these to customers. Five pounds each."

"Okay. I guess these have all the information about the show and actors, yeah?"

"Yes. We're about to open up the auditorium to customers. I'll be on the other side. Only talk to me if there's a problem. I don't want to hear your life story."

"Right. Bye."

India walks away.

Well, that was a fun interaction.

I just stand there, holding a stack of programmes awkwardly.

At least you have a job, Scarlett. Don't worry about making friends just yet.

I glance up at the stage. The curtain is down, revealing nothing behind. It's a proper old proscenium arch.

I whistle in appreciation.

I love this theater.

Soon enough, customers start to stream in towards their seats. I hold the programme high above my head. I even sell a few. I don't get a chance to read through the thing and check out all the actors; I reckon I can do that later.

There's a lot of running around from PR people inside the auditorium. I watch with curiosity as lots of journalists take their seats. It feels like a movie premiere in here.

And then India reappears by my side.

"The show is about to start," she says. "Take your seat. Don't you leave it during the show."

I do.

The theater goes quiet. The auditorium lights dim. My heart rate speeds up.

And then the curtain rises.

I'm too busy being a good little usher scanning the audience for any wayward phones going off that I miss watching the beginning of the show.

But then the actors start to speak.

It's a woman at first. I settle in my seat at the back and

squint at the stage. The actress is very pretty. Long blonde hair. She moves gracefully across the stage.

And then there's an actor that appears next to her. He starts to speak. I'm still scanning over the audience for any lit phone screens.

But I recognize that actor's voice. I know that cut-glass accent.

My body freezes. I let out a gasp. I focus in on the actor.

No. It can't be.

I forget all about being an usher or about the job I have to do. I jump out of my seat and rush into the nearest bathroom, where I open up a programme.

I have to check. I have to make sure. This can't be happening.

I flip through the pages to land on the actors' biographies. This is the best way to find out. Figure out I'm not hallucinating.

But there, clear as day, is the headshot of the man I thought I would never see again. I'm not dreaming. He's smoldering right up at me from the pages of the programme. I would recognize that handsome face anywhere.

He's the main actor in the show. He's right there on stage, not even a hundred yards away from me.

It's Kingsley Heath-Harding.

19

KINGSLEY

STEPPING out onto a West End stage for the first time is the most thrilling moment of my life. It far outweighs any other vices in my life, even girls and sex.

This is the culmination of years of hard work and training. Years of rejections and effort. And now I'm here in a London theater, about to fulfill my lifelong dream.

This play could be the starting role of my acting career. There has been so much media buzz around this part, and especially around me. According to all the papers in London, I'm the *rising talent* of the West End. A star in the making.

Everything is riding on tonight's performance. Anyone who is anyone in the UK arts community is here.

I can't let anything, or anyone, fuck this up for me.

Not in my moment of glory.

And so, I step onto the West End stage in a state of high excitement. I'm ready to take this on. I'm so fucking confident.

I'm young, smart, wealthy, talented, and extremely good-looking. I'm at my very peak.

I say my first line. Perfectly delivered. I glow inside.

Yeah, I'm going to be a star. I'm going to give this crowd the best fucking performance they've ever seen.

I look out into the audience.

And then I see *her*.

Well, I think it's her. I catch a glimpse of that fiery red hair and a quick shot of that pretty face before she disappears, running into a bathroom at the back of the darkened auditorium.

It can't be her. It possibly can't.

But I'm sure it was.

And then I forget my next line.

My co-star, Penelope Jellis, glares at me from across the stage.

Oh. Shit.

My line.

What is it?

Everything goes quiet. Penelope continues to glare at me with a real *I'm going to kill you later* look.

I better stop thinking about Scarlett. It could've been her running to the bathroom, but I really can't worry about that now.

Then it comes back to me. I say my line. Penelope's expression changes back to a smile, and the play continues.

The rest of the show goes by in a wild blur. Lots of lines, lots of words. Luckily, I remember them all, although it does feel like I'm operating on autopilot.

All I can think about is Scarlett Hart.

What is she doing here in London?

Is she even real, or is what I saw a beautiful apparition coming out of my nightmares to haunt me for leaving her? A trick of my mind?

Surely, it can't actually be her. No fucking way.

I mean, she did tell me it was her dream to move to this city, but I never thought she would actually *do* it for real. It has been years. Could it really be her?

The rest of the performance speeds past until I'm pulled from my thoughts by a roar of enthusiastic applause. The end of the show.

I'm bowing right here, in the middle of a West End stage I've thought about for so long holding Penelope's hand, pretending to bask in the adulation of London's glitterati, and yet all I'm thinking of is the American girl I made love to all those years ago.

I scan the clapping audience for Scarlett's red hair, but I can't find it amongst the crowd. My heart drops.

Maybe she was just a ghost.

The curtain falls, and Penelope pulls me into my dressing room. We're both sweating.

And then I remember the performance. The lines I said. Was it even good? I don't know.

My head is spinning.

The stage manager pats me congratulatorily on the back. I feel like I'm in shock.

"Wow," Penelope exclaims when we run into my dressing room. "That was *incredible*."

I fall back into my dressing room chair, only now realizing how exhausted I am.

"Yeah," I reply to her in a tired dazed. "Incredible."

Doesn't feel like it.

Penelope sits down next to me. Like me, she comes from a very wealthy and very posh British family. She's an emerging actress as well. This is also her West End debut. It's like we're different sides of the same coin. Well, that's what others have said to me.

Penelope is glamorous. Classy. She glides through life

with the easy confidence of someone born into money and power. Men get all awestruck over her supermodel looks. Her blonde hair. Her full lips and great tits.

It's been remarked many a time that she and I would make the perfect couple. That we match.

Well, we did fuck. One time. Of course two co-stars would. That's the cliché of the acting business.

But I felt nothing for her.

Not like what I felt for that American girl. No one has come close to Scarlett Hart in four years. Not all the fawning girls I've had come diving willingly into my bed.

"What the fuck was that about?" Penelope asks me.

"Huh?"

"Your weird little pause at the beginning? What the fuck was that?"

Oh. She means the moment I think I saw Scarlett, and I forgot my line.

"Nothing," I reply nonchalantly. "Pausing for dramatic effect."

She eyes me suspiciously. "Well, I wasn't amused."

She rarely is.

"You think it went well?" I asked her.

Penelope reaches out and grips my muscular bicep. "Darling, we were wonderful. We've got such amazing chemistry. We're going to be *stars*. You were so damn sexy up there on stage."

I know that look on her face; I've seen it on a lot of girls. She wants me to kiss her.

As if that's going to happen, especially when I've got Scarlett on my mind.

"Great," I reply.

Penelope shuffles towards me, thrusting her large breasts out so that they push into my arm. Her open lips are close to mine. She gives me a real strong *fuck me* stare, very different from the *I'm going to kill you later* one she gave me on stage. She leans her lips closer to mine. Oh, she is really angling for us to strip naked and fuck right now.

I'm not in the mood at all. My dick isn't even semi-hard.

My dressing room door flies open. In steps Steve, our director. If he notices Penelope and my closeness, he doesn't mention it.

"What the fuck was that pause about?" he asks me.

"Fuck off, Steve," I reply. "How was it?"

He lifts his fingers to his mouth like a French kiss. "*Magnifico.* You two were superb."

"That's all I need to hear," I say as I pull away from Penelope. I hear her groan as her tits lift away from my skin.

"I bet the reviews are going to be amazing," Steve continues. "You two coming to greet the press party? Do some photos? You better be."

"In a minute," I say. "I want some time to decompress."

"I'll stay with you," Penelope pleads.

"I need some time *alone.*"

With a harrumph, she storms out of my dressing room. Steve gives me an eager thumbs up before he leaves as well.

I shut the door after them.

Now I am alone.

I should be over the moon about my performance. I should be fucking Penelope over the chair in this very room right now, keeping the press at bay whilst I cum inside a beautiful woman.

But that sighting of Scarlett Hart can't be erased from my mind.

If she is real, if she really is working here at this theater, then that means one thing.

I have to find her. And - trust me – like that first day at Crystal River's high school, I fucking will.

20

SCARLETT

My heart is pounding, and my head is spinning, but I try to keep in all in control. I just have to get through this front-of-house debrief and *then* I can process who I just saw on stage.

I'm standing in a circle of ushers in the main foyer of the Prestige Theater. We're all waiting for Giles to appear. I don't know any of these people except for India, but she's on the other side of the circle, ignoring me like a bad smell.

Kingsley is here.

I exhale, trying to let out all the tension in my body. It isn't working. I'm freaking out inside.

I spent the rest of the play sitting completely still in my usher seat, watching Kingsley with rising terror. I tried to do my job. I can't lose it on my first night, even if *he's* up there on stage.

I just hope he hasn't seen me. Of course, he couldn't have. He was too busy acting to worry about some usher sitting at the back of the auditorium. It's been too long, anyway. He surely wouldn't recognize me. I was just some girl he fucked and then fucked over four years ago.

And he was *so good*. No wonder he's up there as a star in lights. The man really can act.

And, once upon a time, he was acting in my bedroom. We *kissed* in my bedroom.

Holy shit. That actually happened...

But that was a different life - a different time and place - and I was a very different girl back then.

"How was the show?" Giles asks, appearing out of nowhere to stand in the middle of the circle. "Any problems?"

A couple of the ushers speak, but I can barely listen above the sound of my own heart thumping.

There were some issues with a customer that gets discussed. Something to do with people arriving late. I'm not paying attention.

And then the meeting is over.

"Thank you, everyone," Giles says. "Oh, and all of you are invited to the afterparty. You can bring a plus one. I'll see you there."

The ushers rush to the changing room, chatting about the impending party.

I turn to join them, but then Giles taps me on the shoulder from behind.

"I need to talk to you," he says quietly. Ominously. "*Alone.*"

"Okay, sure."

Giles waits for all the ushers to leave before he speaks. When he does so, he stares at me intensely and with a disapproving frown. Like a principal telling off a naughty student.

"I heard you left the auditorium during the show," he tells me. "Is that true?"

Crap.

India must've told him. I knew I shouldn't have trusted that girl.

I gulp. This could be the end of my job here, and I've not even completed a full shift. I decide to tell the truth.

"Yes, I did."

Giles' frown grows even tighter.

"And why, may I ask?"

Oh, what the hell.

"I recognized one of the actors on stage. I hadn't seen him for a very long time, and I just needed a moment to decompress in the bathroom. Seeing him just... threw me off."

"You know one of the actors?"

"Yeah. Kingsley Heath-Harding."

Giles' face immediately changes into wide-eyed astonishment.

"You know Kingsley? Wow, I'm a big fan of him. You actually know him?"

I have to admit, I'm kinda taken aback by the man's sudden enthusiasm.

"Yeah, he went to my high school for a bit."

"That is amazing. I can't believe you know him. Wow. I've met him at stage door a few times, and he is so nice."

The man has done a complete one-eighty. He's giggly and excited.

"Yeah, he is," I lie. "He's a nice guy."

"I can't believe it. Of course, you should've had a moment to yourself after seeing such a friend."

"Does this mean I can go?"

Giles nods his head.

"Oh, yes. Enjoy the afterparty."

Okay, so somehow I got out of that alive.

I head back up the staircase, but before I make it up the first stair, Giles calls my name.

"Scarlett?"

"Yeah?"

"You will introduce him to me, will you? Kingsley at the afterparty. Properly."

I freeze.

"Uh, yeah. Sure. If he's there."

Giles winks at me. "Thanks."

He lets me go then, and I scramble out of there.

I'm just glad not to have lost my job.

21

SCARLETT

GRACE ARRIVES at the same time as I do, running up to me with a beaming smile on her face.

"Scarlett! Thank you so much for inviting me," she says as she envelops me in a big hug. "I can't believe I'm getting to go to such a fancy party."

If I do see Kingsley tonight at the afterparty, then I *really* don't want to be on my own, and that's why I've invited Grace along as my plus one.

I look at her in shock. She's come in an amazing blue dress that really compliments her eyes.

She looks beautiful.

"Thank you for coming," I reply. I really mean it. I hold on to her tight. "You look stunning."

"So do you."

Grace doesn't know anything about what has happened to me tonight. I just messaged her to say I want her to tag along and to dress up nice. She hasn't disappointed.

"It's so cool that the party is at the actual bloody Tower of London," she says, staring at the fortifications surrounding us. We're at the front gate of the ancient fortress, built a thousand years ago by William the Conqueror to subjugate London after he invaded the country. All these years on, it's still mightily impressive. And, right now, somewhere behind these stone walls, there might be Kingsley lurking in this old castle.

"Shall we go in?" I suggest, leading Grace by the arm past the bouncer and into the main building of the Tower.

For tonight, the place has been decked out to be like a trendy nightclub. Dark, with cool lighting. Waitresses are walking around offering guests tall glasses of champagne on silver trays.

"Oh, yes please," Grace enthusiastically says as she collects two glasses for us from the waitress by the door. We chink them together and giggle, amazed at the crazy situation we've found ourselves in.

"Two hours ago, I was in my pajamas on my sofa," Grace says. "Now I'm here. I'm so glad I've got you to be my glamourous friend."

"This is most certainly a one-off," I tell her. "My life is usually not this glamorous, trust me."

I look around the historic castle all dressed up for an exclusive VIP party, and I can't believe my luck. A few days ago, I was thinking I might be homeless in this city, and now I'm at the *freaking* Tower of London with my new best friend being treated as guests of the hottest new play in town.

"Wow, look at all this cool stuff," Grace says as she points to a row of medieval armor hanging from the walls. Gleaming swords and spears next to expensive canapés for the party. "This place is real fancy."

"It sure is."

"I feel like a fraud being here. Who let the riff-raff in?"

"Well, don't feel like a fraud. We both deserve this," I say. "Let's drink all of their champagne. It is free, after all."

"Scarlett, you don't have to tell me twice. I'm way ahead of you."

We wander around the main area of the afterparty. I recognize a few of the ushers I worked with. There are also a lot of celebrities here. Some from films, some supermodels. Grace and I stare, open-mouthed, at them. All stunning, otherworldly people literally walking around us.

The whole time I keep my eyes open for a certain tall, gorgeous man, but I don't find him. That's good. I grip onto Grace tightly. I don't want to lose her, but then I do feel like I urgently need to go and pee.

As if on cue, Grace turns to me.

"I'm super hungry. You don't mind if I go over there and gobble the canapés?" she asks, gesturing at a table full of little dishes.

"No, you go ahead. I need to use the bathroom."

"I'll see you in a minute."

"Sure."

We part in our different ways. I head straight for the ladies while Grace makes a beeline for the snacks.

There's no one else inside the bathroom. I sit down and do my pee before going over to the sink to check out my face.

Someone walks in and stands at the sink next to mine. I glance over. It's the main actress from the show. I think her name is Penelope... *something*? She was really good. She has such a nice voice, really refined like Kingsley's. She's also even more incredibly beautiful in person. Her blonde hair is to die for. She has the most luscious lips.

God, I am really no match for a specimen like her.

122

I don't know if it's the glass of champagne I just quickly washed down or the fact that this woman knows Kingsley that makes me start to speak.

"I just saw you on stage. You were amazing. Are you having a nice night?"

Penelope just turns to face me, slowly. She scans me up and down as if reviewing my body. Then she scoffs and walks directly out of the bathroom without a reply.

Okay.

Rude.

I shake my head. Some of these people really think they operate in another world, don't they?

Maybe I should just head back to the flat. I clearly don't belong here.

I step out of the bathroom to see Grace by the canapés table. She's chatting with some guy. I say chatting, I mean *flirting*. She resting an arm on his shoulder and is laughing at all his jokes. She looks like she's having fun, so I won't bother her.

Instead, I wander aimlessly down a hallway away from the party. Suits of armor stand at guard around me.

I walk into a wide room, even darker than the main party area. Right in the middle of the room is an illuminated glass cage, and inside that cage are the Crown Jewels of the United Kingdom. They're resting on plush cushions, proudly being displayed. This is the very crown the Queen wore when she was coronated back in the fifties. I inspect the cage. It must be under so much security.

So much history and tradition in one place. I wonder what it'll be like to put that crown on your head. I wonder what it would feel like to be a queen.

I know it seems to happen to me every few hours, but once again I'm blown away by the thought that I'm actually here in London.

Man, I love this city.

I feel like I'm alone, but then I hear footsteps approaching from behind. I spin around on the spot.

And that's when I see Kingsley Heath-Harding coming straight for me.

22

KINGSLEY

"Hello Queen," I say to the girl I've been looking for all night.

Scarlett flinches at the nickname, but she stares me down with a *fuck you* look, which has the opposite effect she's thinking of and just looks really cute on her.

I smile. She's actually real. She's actually in front of me. *She's all mine.*

"You."

She points aggressively at me. Aw, she looks *even more* cute now that she's absolutely fuming at me. I want to lean down and kiss that sexy, pouting mouth of hers.

We're alone, and I'm turned on. Nothing's going to stop me.

"Nice dress," I remark, making sure she notices my eyes scanning down to her cleavage. She crosses her arms, trying to cover her body from my prying gaze.

Oh, she's absolutely *furious* now. Exactly the way I

want her. I like prodding her like this. It's better for her to feel something for me than nothing at all.

"What do you want, Kingsley? Why are you here, talking to me?"

"I thought I saw you from the stage. Are you working at the Prestige? Is that how you've managed to score tickets to the press party?"

She doesn't reply to my questions.

"What do you want, Kingsley?"

"I guess I'm wondering what you thought of my performance. Was I good?"

Pause.

Again, Scarlett doesn't answer my question.

"What. Do. You. Want. Kingsley."

Ignoring her demands, I slowly take my time and scan over the rest of her. She looks older - more mature - but she is still the same girl I remember. That blazing hair. Those sparkling eyes. That milky skin. Memories of my fingers deep in her pussy come flooding back to me with a sudden intensity.

I remember her moans of pleasure. How could I possibly erase those sounds from my mind?

But tonight, her sassiness is on full display. I know I'm going to have to work extra hard to get back into her pants.

This is definitely going to take all my effort.

She holds unblinking eye contact with me, demanding an answer. I like her backbone. It's been a long time since anyone has ever stood up to Kingsley Heath-Harding like this.

"You've actually made it here, Scarlett. You followed your dreams. You're in London."

"I know."

"You acting?"

"No, I gave that up a long time ago," she says. "I'm a terrible actor. Always have been."

"You were pretty convincing to me back in high school."

"If anyone is a good actor here, then it's you," Scarlett replies curtly. "Pretending to like a girl, then to just disappear and break her heart? Oscar-worthy performance, I must say."

I mime being wounded in my heart. "Ouch. That cuts me deep, Scarlett."

"You can leave now, Kingsley."

Despite the venom in her voice, I can sense she doesn't really want me to leave.

She's curious about me. She wants to find out more. I bet she's missed me as much as I've missed her. There's too much of a spark flying between us for her to let me go just yet.

And I have no plans of leaving the woman I've been thinking about all night.

I move even closer to her. She doesn't resist, but she still continues to shoot daggers at me from her bright green eyes.

"Remember, Scarlett, I prefer to be called *King*."

She shakes her head dismissively at my comment, but even so, she takes a step forward to bring us even closer.

We're so intimate now. Only a few inches separate our skin from touching. I can smell her. A sweet perfume that takes me back to that week in America. Man, I am holding back my desire to bend her over right here, right now, and fuck her the way I know she wants me to.

Keep your pants on, King.

My cock twitches. I am so hard.

"I'm not ever going to call you by that cheesy name," she says. "Never."

I'm not the kind of guy to hear the word *no* come from the lips of a girl. No girl has wanted to refuse my advances for a very long time, if ever. Scarlett's defiance somehow turns me on even more.

"That fiery spark, just like your hair, I've *missed* that," I reply as I reach out with my hand and hold Scarlett's chin with the tips of my fingers. Her lips quiver with anticipation, and she doesn't back away. I've got her just where I want her. "Only you can say *no* to me. That's how I know it's *you*."

I lean forward, aiming straight for that pretty open mouth of hers.

"It is me," she whispers, succumbing to my unflinching advance.

"So, what did you think of my performance tonight?"

"You know I'm not going to answer that question, Kingsley."

"Please do."

"Nope."

"You do know that I've been thinking of you ever since that night."

The tension is thick as our lips brush.

But before I can kiss her properly, she pushes me back with her hands on my chest.

"If you've been thinking so hard about that night," she retorts forcefully. "If you've been lusting after me that hard, then why didn't you come back for me?"

The question throws me. I step back.

She really wants an answer? Right now?

I open my mouth to speak, but there's a sudden tap on my shoulder.

Scarlett looks behind me. I turn to see Ben Helper – my personal publicist - who whispers into my ear.

"You gotta go back to the party, King. There's press to see you."

I nod. "Wait one moment," I tell him before facing Scarlett. "This is Ben, my publicist."

She doesn't seem impressed. She does not care at all about me being a rich celebrity being hounded by people looking for an interview. That's something other people are obsessed with, but not Scarlett. I like the balls on her.

"Hello," she grudgingly greets my publicist.

"Be quick," Ben tells me before dashing back into the party.

"What does he want?" Scarlett asks.

I scoff. "Why do you want to know?"

She crosses her arms again. "I don't."

"So, tell me, Scarlett. Have you been following me? Is that why you work at the Prestige Theater?"

"*Following you?*" She snorts derisively. "Trust me, I didn't know you were an actor in the show. If I had done, I would've run in the opposite direction. I actually can't believe I'm still here talking to you."

"But you're here, aren't you? If you really didn't want to see me again, then you wouldn't have come to this press party, wouldn't you?"

She's fuming now, but I know I've got her with that question.

She secretly wants me.

"Kingsley..."

"So, are we going to see each other again?" I ask her quickly.

Before Scarlett can answer, someone else interrupts us. Some drunk guy. He staggers over. I think I've met him before. I recognize him from somewhere.

"Hello, Scarlett," he says. I eye him suspiciously. I don't want trouble. I'm ready to fight this dude off if Scarlett wants me to, but she seems alright with him.

Who is this asshole?

129

I hate being interrupted.

"Hello, Giles," she replies.

"Are you going to introduce me?" the man asks her, slurring his words.

"Yes. Kingsley, this is Giles Bonner, the theater manager of the Prestige."

Right.

He offers me a sweaty hand. I shake it.

"Hello, Giles."

"Big fan," he shouts in my direction. "Really big fan of you."

"Thank you."

Get lost, prick. Can't you see I'm talking to the girl of my dreams?

Scarlett's face goes the color of her name. She's embarrassed by her boss. I like that.

"You're really good on stage," Giles continues. "You're going to be the biggest actor in the country, I bet."

"That's the game plan."

"Then I can tell everyone I know that I've met the great Kingsley Heath-Harding."

"Sure."

Scarlett is really embarrassed now. I give her a smile. Oh, I'm enjoying this immensely.

"Thanks for hiring this girl, Giles."

"She started today."

I look at Scarlett. "Did she?"

"Yeah," she says.

"You're not going to regret hiring her, Giles. Trust me."

"Stop talking, Kingsley," Scarlett says.

"How about I give you a tour backstage sometime?" I ask her cheekily.

But before Scarlett can deliver another one of her barbs, we're interrupted by yet *another* person.

God, can I not just flirt with this girl in peace?

This time a girl that must be the same age as Scarlett and I comes bounding over. She's pretty, with black hair and bright blue eyes. She completely ignores Giles and me and practically jumps on the American girl.

"Scarlett, I've been looking everywhere for you. You wouldn't believe the conversation I've just had. You would've found it hilarious. This guy wanted to chat me up, right, but then I accidentally spilled my drink all over him. You should've seen his face! What a boner killer."

Scarlett laughs, and I'm jealous that I'm not the one who's making her.

Giles just stares blankly. He's so pissed.

This new girl is a whirlwind of passion. I like her. Like Scarlett, she also doesn't give a fuck about me. She's got me interested. My eyes are only for Scarlett, though.

"Who's this guy?" she asks Scarlett, frowning at me.

"Grace," Scarlett says. "This is Kingsley."

"Hello," I say. I like how Scarlett is seemingly having to introduce me to everyone she knows.

Grace is squinting at my face. "Hi! Do I know you? I feel like we've met before."

I know I've never seen this girl in my entire life.

"No, I don't think so," I reply. "I definitely would've remembered you if I had."

She continues staring at my face.

"Well, you look kinda familiar."

23

SCARLETT

"I DEFINITELY DO KNOW him from somewhere," Grace tells me.

We walk in the darkness, our way only lit by dim street-lamps and the glittering London skyline. The pavement feels cold on my bare feet. Both Grace and I have removed our heels when we left the Tower so that we could walk easier and quicker.

"Maybe you've seen him on a poster for his play on the Tube or something," I reply to my friend.

Grace doesn't seem convinced. "Maybe."

"It's such a beautiful view," I say, nodding out towards the Thames. I want to change the subject away from Kings-ley. The tall skyscrapers of the city rise up on the other side of the water like modern-day versions of the Tower of London. St Paul's Cathedral sits nestled among them. A skyline that's thousands of years old but has changed a million times.

"I'll never get tired of it," Grace says. She runs over to

the wall above the rushing river below us and climbs on top. She's standing on the wall, skipping along it like a trapeze artist.

"Woah," I nervously caution. "Be careful."

She blows a raspberry at me. "I'm perfectly fine, Scarlett. Come and join me. It's fun."

She offers her hand to help me up, but I refuse. "If you fall into the Thames, don't rely on me to jump in there and save you."

"Get up here, Scarlett. Feel the wind flowing through your hair."

I laugh and shake my head. "I can feel the wind from down here, thank you very much."

Grace lifts her arms above her head, closes her eyes, and sighs. "We're young, we're alive, and we're in London," she shouts out across the city.

"And we're also *drunk*," I reply. "It's not safe."

"Okay, help me down then."

Grace jumps off the wall and onto the pavement, held by my helping hands.

"You alright?" I ask her.

"That was amazing."

"And dangerous."

We continue walking away from the Tower of London towards the Tube. The city is empty and quiet. No one else is around. My head spins from all the free champagne we drank.

"I'm so happy we've found each other," Grace says, wrapping her arm around my waist and bringing me in close to her.

"Me too. You've saved me from homelessness."

"I think we're gonna have the best time living together."

"Yep, I think that too."

"Two London ladies."

"Oh, yes."

We keep walking around the corner.

"Is everything okay?" Grace asks me inquisitively. "Are you alright?"

"Yeah. Why?"

She senses something's up.

"What's wrong?"

I think about Kingsley. About the man I thought was gone forever, and how he turned up again tonight like a lightning bolt.

He didn't try to make excuses or even act the slightest bit embarrassed about seeing me tonight.

He looked dangerous. Like he was ready to break my heart again. The man wants me, but I'm not going to be that easy for him.

And he also looked gorgeous. Even more refined and handsome than he was a few years ago. He's certainly a man that knows how to wear a suit.

I hated him, and yet I couldn't take my eyes off him the entire time. His body. His jaw. His eyes. My own body was so submissive to his delicate touch as he held my chin and angled for my lips, and I hate how much he turns me on. I shouldn't be so responsive to him, but I can't help it.

Damn, I have to admit, the man has a hold on me.

A really strong hold.

I know I won't stop dreaming about him for a very long time. He had existed so long in my memory. Half-real. Like he'd been something I'd made up. So to see him close to me – to practically hear the actual *beating* of his heart – made my poor head spin.

I miss Kingsley. That much is true. That low and sexy voice of his.

After I introduced him to Grace, she pulled me away from him before the man and I could chat privately again.

I'm glad she did, otherwise I might've done something stupid like fall for his charms. I might've disappeared with my friend, but I know he wants to see me again. And Kingsley Heath-Harding doesn't seem like the type of man to give up chasing after something he wants.

"What's wrong?" Grace asks me again.

"Nothing," I reply, trying to erase from my mind the exciting memory of tasting Kingsley's cock between my lips. "I think I've just seen a ghost, that's all."

24

KINGSLEY

THE REVIEWS for my West End debut are good.

Like, real fucking good.

Five stars all around.

My theater dressing room is filled with flowers for my performance. Lots of flowers. Delivered from everyone with a name in London.

I guess I should be flattered. I guess I should be over the fucking moon with getting this level of recognition from London's best, brightest, and people with enough money to buy their way into that elite world.

But the only thing on my mind is a certain girl with stunning red hair.

Her soft, wet lips as they brushed mine. Her steely look, with a smoldering pit of desire behind her eyes. I want to caress her hair and feel her hot breath against my skin.

I think of her naked body lying between my very own bedsheets.

It's impossible to deny that I can't get Scarlett Hart from out my head.

There's even a letter from my father sitting on my dressing room table, but even his approval of my West End debut can't redirect my focus away from Scarlett.

Fuck me.

I decide to open his letter. Anything to get my mind off that girl.

It's been typed up, not written, and that's how I know it's not actually *from* him. Probably some secretary in some backroom wrote it. But, hey, I don't care. I've gotten over my father's eternal absence from my life years ago. The only people whose opinions I respect are Camilla and my brother's.

Speaking of Duke, it's at the moment right after I finish reading "father's" letter that I get a phone call from my brother.

"Hey man," he says, his deep voice echoing down the line.

"Duke. How's it going?"

"I'm just giving you a call to say I'm looking forward to tomorrow night."

"And what's happening tomorrow night?"

"I'm coming to watch your show," he says.

"You don't have to do that," I reply.

"Of course I do. You're my little bro. I'm seeing everything you do."

"I bet Father isn't going to make an appearance," I say.

Duke sighs. "No, I don't think he will. He knows how important this is for you, but he won't even show up."

"Yep."

"You gotta prepare yourself for that. We both do. He's never going to show up."

"I know."

"Oh well. Screw him. I'm going to be Lord Heath-Harding when he shuffles off this mortal coil, and there's nothing he can do to stop that."

I laugh. "Yeah, he'll *hate* that. He'll be turning in his grave."

"Yes, he will."

My brother cheers me up. We've both got each other, and that feels good. Family runs thicker than blood and all that.

After Duke hangs up, I fall down in my chair and absentmindedly flick through the *congratulations* cards on my dressing room table.

I'm thinking of Scarlett.

About how I had to leave her and America four years ago. That was hard. Would Scarlett even believe I left because Father changed his mind about America and packed me back to the UK with just a click of his fingers? I doubt Scarlett could possibly understand my world and my father's power. Normal people don't have a noble family name that stretches back hundreds of years.

He changed his mind and wanted me to go to Oxford instead of an Ivy League college. He didn't succeed, though. I never went to Oxford. I defied his wishes and became an actor.

It's the only act of defiance I've committed against my father, and it's cost me his presence in my life.

But now Scarlett blames me for abandoning her, and deep down, I know she has every right to think that. I *could've* resisted Father better. I *could've* insisted on staying in America with Scarlett. I didn't.

But now is my chance to make things right again.

She's the one girl that's been on my mind for this long, no matter what other girls have come into my life. It's always been *her*.

I want her back.

And Kingsley Heath-Harding always gets what he wants.

The door to my dressing room bangs open, and Penelope swans in like she owns the place. She does not knock. Typical dominating Penelope.

"Oh my god, King, have you seen these reviews?"

She's holding aloft a newspaper which proudly announces five gold stars for our production.

"I have."

"We're going to be stars," Penelope replies, her face dazzling in visions of her Hollywood future.

"We'll see," I say.

Despite my humble facade, I fucking *know* I'm going to be the next best thing.

Penelope slowly strolls over to me and sits in my lap, her legs around my thighs so that she's facing me. Her hands make their teasing way up my arms. I know what she wants.

"We'll both be stars," she says, bringing her perfectly tanned face close to mine before pulling out her phone. "I'll read one to you. See, this one says we have amazing chemistry. I think we do. We have perfect chemistry. Do you think so too?"

"Yep. Sure."

She licks her lips seductively at me.

"We're going to win loads of awards. I'm excited about doing it all with you. As more than colleagues."

"Penelope, we're just actors playing characters," I reply, removing her fingers from sensually rubbing my firm chest.

"Our chemistry is just for the stage."

Penelope pouts.

"You weren't like this the other week, King."

Yeah, that was before press night. Before I saw that girl in the audience.

"That was one time," I reply.

We slept together once, and I am going to keep it that way.

"Oh, King."

"I'm going to get ready for tonight's show," I say, practically telling her to piss off.

Penelope senses it. She frowns.

And then she stands up and steps back.

"You're boring," she says spitefully. Her words don't hurt at all.

I say nothing back. I've turned away a lot of girls before. I'm a pro at pushing a girl out of my bed.

Then she walks out of my dressing room, leaving me alone to think about Scarlett. To think about me finding her again and going up to her to claim what's mine. Kissing her soft lips.

I really can't get the girl out of my head, and there's only one person I can see to speak about this. The woman who raised me.

25

KINGSLEY

THE GATE OPENS, and I drive my Aston Martin slowly through past the walls of the estate. I guide my car around the beautiful stone fountain until I'm parking right outside the giant Victorian-era front doors. It's a place I've been to many times, and somewhere that stirs a particular emotion in me every time I see it. I'm always transported back to my childhood when I'm here. *My lonely childhood.*

It's the Heath-Harding manor house. My family's country mansion.

It's a magnificent old building situated in the middle of green fields in the very middle of England. Today's bright sunshine illuminates the marble columns outside the mansion. My family has owned this place, and all the acres of land surrounding it, for hundreds of years. It's our traditional family seat.

And one day my brother and I will inherit it. And then, one day, pass it onto our own children. They will pass it onto theirs, and so on. Continuing the Heath-Harding name for generations to come.

But I prefer London, and its hustle and bustle, to the quiet of the country. I've barely been back here since leaving home properly at eighteen to make my name in the big smoke. I don't really like this place, but today I'm here to see someone I need to see.

I step out of my shiny Aston Martin dressed in my favorite suit - tailored in Savile Row, naturally - and step up to the imposing front doors.

My father has offered me a full-time personal driver, but I prefer to drive myself. I want to move away from the spoiled lifestyle. I want to be my own man.

The front doors to the mansion open. Camilla is waiting behind them like she can somehow sense my arrival. That woman knows me too well.

"Camilla," I greet.

She regards me with her trademark strict expression.

She's the person I'm here to see.

"Kingsley."

She may appear to be a stiff matriarch, but even she can't hide the affection for me behind her voice. "Long time no see."

"Well, theater is dominating all my time these days, naturally."

"Hm. And not the temptations of London that I read about in the tabloids?"

"You're the only temptation I need, Camilla," I say boyishly as I give her a peck on the cheek.

"I doubt that," she replies.

"I didn't take you as someone who reads the tabloids, Camilla. I thought they'd be beneath you."

"When it's the only way to keep up with you, then I

read them. You've been on a lot of adventures lately, I've seen. Your love life is splashed out all over page two."

"All lies, Camilla. All lies and gossip."

She scoffs quietly, not believing me. "Come on in. I've got the kettle on."

We head into a small dining room, one of five in the building, and sit at the table while Camilla pours the tea. Hanging inside the main entrance of the mansion is an immense chandelier worth millions. The manor house's decor is of a palace. On the walls hang portraits of long-dead ancestors, all staring imposingly at you as you walk past. In every room seems to be historical artifacts. Candelabra from revolutionary France. Diamonds from India. Statues from ancient Greece. Our mansion could rival the British Museum with its collection.

"How have you been, Camilla?" I ask her as she passes me a cup of tea.

Camilla has been living at the manor house on her own. Well, other than the army of gardeners and grounds-people employed to maintain the estate. Father rarely visits this place.

"You know me, King," Camilla replies with a wink. "I'm always fine."

"As I've said a billion times before, you are more than welcome to come stay with me in London. I have enough space for a circus to stay in my penthouse."

"Oh, I don't like the madness of that city. I prefer it here."

"Okay, then. But the offer is always open."

"I appreciate that," Camilla says, taking a long sip of tea. "So, why have you come here today? What's on your mind?"

I sigh. She really knows me.

And now it's time to talk to her about what I came here for.

I take in a deep breath.

"You remember America?"

Camilla rolls her eyes. "Of course I do. That awful place."

"You know how we left overnight because of Father's orders?"

"Yes. I remember it was very stressful. I'm glad all that business is over with."

"Well, there was a girl there. An American girl I had to leave behind."

Camilla takes another sip of tea and eyes me. "I suspected as much."

Of course she did.

"I never got the chance to say goodbye to her. Truth be told, I was afraid I'd left it too late to even contact her. I was terrified to tell her I had moved back to the other side of the world."

"And so you broke her heart, didn't you?" she asks me.

I tut. "Yeah. I think so."

"So why are you coming to me now about this?" Camilla asks. "It was four years ago."

"Well, that's the crazy part. She's turned up here. In London."

"Oh."

"And we met the other night. She's working at the same theater I'm performing at."

There's a loud clink as Camilla places her cup down on the saucer. "And you've spoken to her?"

"Yep."

"And how is she about the whole, you know, *breaking her heart*?"

"Not very well."

"I thought so. You want to see her again?"

I take a pause before arriving at an answer I know is the absolute truth. "Yes."

"But you're the son of a Lord," she tells me. "A penniless American girl would not be the preferred choice of partner for you by any means, even in this progressive modern age. Your father would disapprove. It'll be tradition for you to find some aristocratic English girl."

"Oh, I know that."

"You would have to fight him tooth and nail about this."

"Yes."

"He won't just let you have this girl without a fight. You might even lose your inheritance, you understand that?"

"I know that, Camilla. But I don't care. I want her."

"I hate having to repeat myself, but it is tradition for you to marry a member of the British aristocracy, not some American girl."

"Yep."

"But," Camilla says slowly. "*Fuck* tradition."

I nearly snort out tea from my nose. "Camilla? I've never heard you swear. Never."

"Listen to me, King," she says, her voice lowering to a serious whisper. "Follow your heart. I've watched you grow up; I've *helped* you grow up. I've seen you through all storms, and if there's one piece of advice I can give you, it's this. Your biggest regrets in life come from when you don't follow your heart. Trust me."

"I do trust you, Camilla. You've been like a mother to me."

"You know, seeing you talk like this... you're different. Changed. Matured." Camilla leans closer to me, still maintaining her perfect posture. "You know that when you talk like this, you remind me of your mother. I used to sit here in this very spot and talk to her for hours about matters of the heart. She was strong in love, you know. Happy. She once made a choice to follow her heart instead of her head and so she married your father. She never regretted that decision. I see that same spark in you I saw in her as you sit here now. Your mother didn't let her love go to waste, and neither should you, King. If you want this girl, then go after her with everything you got. That's what your mother would've done."

I nod slowly. Camilla knew my mother well, but she's rarely opened up about her. It's nice to hear something about the woman I barely remember.

It's nice to know she was like me.

"Thanks, Camilla," I reply softly. "That helps a lot."

"So," she replies, leaning back against her chair and picking up her tea again. "What are you going to do?"

26

SCARLETT

I TRY to keep my eyes off Kingsley, but it's so hard when he's just *right there*.

On stage.

Whilst I have to work.

I have to sit in the theater's auditorium and watch the man who I once fell for *hard* stand there and perform for nearly three hours. Has there been a more heart-breaking situation for someone to be put under? I seriously doubt it.

I try to scan the audience for any phone lights going off, to spot anyone trying to take prohibited photos, but I can't resist shooting a glance back to the stage. At Kingsley.

Being this close to him – watching him work - makes me want to leave this job, but I can't. That's the annoying thing. This is the one job I've somehow managed to secure here in London and I can't afford to lose it. Not now when I have to start paying rent to Grace.

India is on the other side of the auditorium. She's not

been friendly to me at all, despite my constant attempts to be smiley towards her.

Kingsley strolls across the stage, delivering a monologue. He's a talented actor, there's absolutely no doubt. He's got such a smooth voice that makes my heart soar. He has such a command of the stage like a true pro. Despite how pissed off I am at him, I just want to melt in his gaze. Every move he makes reminds me of that night when he came to my house and fucked me in my bedroom and called me his *good girl*. It's a night I can't forget.

It's pretty horny to see someone have so much unbridled passion for what they do. To be so goddamn talented. It's seductive and is a major freaking turn-on.

But why does it have to be him?

Of course, the moment I came home from the press party I jumped onto my computer and googled that man like a possessed stalker. It's good that he's a celebrity because there's so much information to find out about him available right there on the net. Even stuff about his personal life. It seems like the British tabloids love digging up dirt on the actor, and I'm their eager customer. There are articles about him going on dates with supermodels. Olympian athletes. It seems like he's slept through most of the famous women under the age of thirty in the UK. It made me sick thinking of all those gorgeous women he's had.

And then there's me. The nerdy and socially inept American girl.

The article that sticks in my mind was one about him and his co-star on stage. Penelope Jellis. The one who scoffed at me in the bathroom at the party. Oh, I remember her vividly. There was a photo of them together, leaving a hotel after a day of interviews. The article gushed about them.

· · ·

THEIR CHEMISTRY *on stage is overpowering, and I'm sure it spills over into real life. I can hear wedding bells now. Can you just imagine how gorgeous (and wealthy) their children would be?*

SEEING all the women he's dated makes my heart drop. I cannot compete with these gorgeous people. I'm not on that level at all.

But he did show interest in me. Once.

And again, at the press party.

What does he see in me?

I feel so much lust for Kingsley as I sit there in the darkened theater. There's a pleasurable tightness between my legs as I watch him effortlessly act on stage. My body wants him, even if my mind is dead-set against the thought.

Whilst my focus is on Kingsley, I don't see the customer leaving the auditorium until it's too late. She goes out the side exit that I should be blocking.

Oh, God.

She slips out, and I chase after her, hoping it's not too late to catch her before she accidentally leaves the theater.

Oh, shit.

But when I pass through the curtain, she's there.

And she's not alone.

Giles is standing by the exit, talking to her. My theater manager looks up at me as I enter, but doesn't acknowledge my presence.

"Follow me to the bathroom," he tells the customer before leading her back inside. As he passes me, he ominously whispers into my ear. "See me in my office later."

I've fucked up. Big time.

That's all he says, but it's enough of a threat to make my throat dry.

Have I lost my job on only my second shift?

* * *

I STEP INTO GILES' office after the debriefing at the end of the shift. All the other ushers have gone home. It's just him and me now.

Time to face the music.

The manager doesn't offer me a seat.

"Scarlett," Giles starts, staring up at me from his desk. "Do you see this on the wall?"

He gestures behind him at a framed certificate.

BEST WEST END THEATER MANAGER.

"YEP," I reply.

"I got that award last year because I am *the* best theater manager in the West End. Period. Do you see these photos?"

He points at a collage of images on the wall next to the award. Photos of Giles with famous actors and actresses. So many photos. He looks overjoyed in every single one.

"Yeah," I reply, leaning forward towards the wall. "You have an impressive collection here."

I don't see of photo of him with Kingsley. I guess he hasn't had the chance to ambush him yet.

Giles sighs. "I got them because I really am good at my job. I've worked hard to get to this position. I meet every actor who steps onto this stage. I make sure my theater runs as the best theater in the whole of London, you understand?"

"I do."

"Then I assume you'd agree that I should remove any dead wood," he replies. "That I should get rid of anything that's holding my theater back? So, Scarlett, why should I not fire you?"

I gulp. I sensed something like that was coming.

"I am sorry about earlier, Giles. It won't happen again."

"And your disappearance yesterday during the press show?"

"It will not happen again, I promise."

Giles pauses, frowning at me. "Scarlett, this is your final warning."

Where have I heard that before? Oh, right. London Bridge.

I'm starting to think that maybe I'm just a terrible employee.

"One more screw-up and you're gone, understood?"

"You're giving me another chance?"

"One more."

"Thank you, Giles," I say.

Phew.

"Okay. Good. No more screw-ups, Scarlett," Giles replies. I nod. "Well, we're the last two people here in the theater. We'll go out the side door and I'll lock up."

I follow him out of the building. We open up a side fire door, and who is waiting for us just outside the door?

Kingsley Heath-Harding.

Of course he is.

"Scarlett Hart," the actor growls in his rough timbre. All the air in my lungs rushes out of my mouth when I spot his perfect body in his tight, expensive suit stroll confidently towards Giles and me.

"Oh, hello Mr. Heath-Harding," my theater manager exclaims, evidently as star-struck as he was by the gorgeous actor as he was last night. "Such a surprise to see you."

Kingsley acts like Giles doesn't even exist. His blue eyes beam into me as he steps up to us. I can smell him from here. His cinnamon-tinged fancy aftershave. My legs wobble under me. I am not prepared to see him like this, still dressed in my sweaty work uniform. But if he is bothered by my appearance, he doesn't show it in the slightest. In fact, he stares at me like he's a predator who wants to devour me.

And I actually might want him to.

"I want to meet you for tea," Kingsley commands me without a hint of hesitation. He's completely unfazed. He's so confident in his order it's like he hasn't even contemplated that I might dare reject it.

"What? *Tea*?"

"Tomorrow. At the London Grand Hotel. At midday."

"Why?" I blurt out.

"I want to talk about things."

"Do I have a choice?" I ask, folding my arms. "Can I say no?"

Kingsley smirks, like I'm speaking nonsense. "Sure, you can say no. But that would be very... *disappointing*."

The way he says that word. Full of desire for me. I can barely speak.

"Maybe I should disappoint you," I reply with venom. Kingsley doesn't even flinch.

Giles' head turns from me to Kingsley, watching this intense interaction with mouth agape.

"You will be there, Scarlett," Kingsley says.

"Is that a threat?"

Kingsley doesn't respond.

Instead, he winks at me and walks away towards an

elegant and very expensive-looking Aston Martin parked across the street.

Oh. That's his car.

He must've been waiting for me for the last hour after the show had finished, waiting to catch me like this. Waiting to ask me out for tea. At the fucking London Grand Hotel.

What the hell is happening?

"You really think you're a James Bond type, don't you?" I call out to Kingsley. He turns around.

Got your attention there, haven't I, Mister Wannabe-Bond?

"What?" he asks, blinking.

Oh, I've really got you there. Good.

"You think you're so damn cool when really you're just a big boy driving and pretending to be some made-up movie character."

Again, Kingsley doesn't seem affected by my vicious comment. He smiles slyly.

"Well, I do drive an Aston Martin," he says calmly and confidently. "I am incredibly handsome, charming, irresistible, and I *always* get the girl."

If I could roll my eyes even further into the back of my head, I would. "So, you think that makes me a Bond girl?"

"No," Kingsley replies slowly. "You're a King girl."

"I ain't nobody's girl."

And then Kingsley *winks* at me, and I feel my blood boiling.

"We'll see."

Fucking we'll see...

He slides into the driver's seat of his car and shuts the door. He won't be able to hear me now even if I yelled at him, and I am *so close* to screaming his stupid name.

"I can't believe you really know Kingsley Heath-Harding," Giles says as soon as Kingsley reaches his car. Giles' whole stern theater manager demeanor has gone, replaced by a thirsty fanboy. I'm astonished at his transformation by just being in close proximity to a celebrity. "And he asked you to the *London Grand Hotel* for tea? Wow."

Ugh.

I hate how my boss was witness to all of that. Kingsley knew *exactly* what he was doing asking me on that date in front of Giles.

His Aston Martin roars into life and speeds off down the street.

"Yeah, he's alright," I say, blushing. I still can't get over how close that beautiful man was to me. I know I should hate him with every fiber of my being for running away without saying a word to me, but my body naturally acts otherwise.

My pussy is practically *leaking* through my panties.

"Are you going to see him tomorrow, then?" Giles asks me. "You should definitely see him for tea."

I bite my lip. Even I have to admit that being chased like this is a pretty major turn-on.

"We'll see," I reply to my boss. "We'll see."

27

SCARLETT

THE FIRST THOUGHT I have when I arrive at the London Grand Hotel is that the British *really know how to do fancy*.

The second thought I have is of how I really feel like I definitely do not belong here in this luxury hotel.

The place is so intimidating. Old and fabulous. Right next to Green Park in the center of London, it makes you feel so small if you're not some wealthy heiress, or at the very least, the owner of a Lamborghini. The place doesn't even need to advertise its services; everyone knows the hotel's name. Everyone *important*, that is. I love it from the first sight.

The doors are held open for me by the immaculately dressed footman who tips his top hat to me in that polite way I've come to expect from Brits. I gulp in terror and nod back at him.

We Americans certainly can't do posh like this.

I step into the long, elegant bar of the hotel. A man who

looks like the maître-d flags me down and hurries across to greet me.

"Hello, madam," he says.

Like the footman outside, he is dressed in a spotless uniform. He's wearing a full tuxedo. I feel like I've stepped back in time to the Victorian age.

And I feel super under-dressed compared to him.

"Hello," I squeak out, nervous. "I'm here for tea."

The maître-d raises an inquisitive eyebrow.

"For tea? You're American?"

"Um, yes."

I don't know what my nationality has to do with anything, but the maître-d flinches at my accent.

"Have you made a reservation?" he asks.

"I don't know. It might be under my friend's name."

"Hm."

The man regards me with a snobby look. I know he's checking out my casual attire, and he clearly does not like what he sees. I didn't come expecting to dress so formally. I guess he thinks I must be some peasant off the streets who has wandered into this luxury palace by mistake, which I *basically* am.

One thing's for sure, the London Grand Hotel is very different from London Bridge back home.

"Maybe I can have a look around for him?" I ask, stuttering.

The maître-d sighs as if I've suggested the worst thing in the world.

I knew coming here today was a bad mistake.

"We don't allow people to "look around" for guests. Maybe you should leave," he suggests passive-aggressively.

That's it. I'm not welcome here.

He's right. I better go.

It really was dumb of me to come today, expecting to see

Kingsley. Just because he sexily growled a command at me last night does not mean I should've actually tried to come here. I've been such an idiot thinking that he was actually being serious. I bet this is all some elaborate joke.

But then, as I'm about to turn and run out the front doors, Kingsley suddenly appears behind the maître-d. He's looking drop-dead gorgeous, as always. Now, this is a man who fits into the dramatic and beautiful interior of the London Grand Hotel.

"Everything alright, Scarlett?" he asks me with all his charming swagger, completely ignoring the maître-d.

"I was just looking for you," I squeak.

"Ah, Mr. Heath-Harding," the maître-d changes his composure. He's practically bowing apologetically now. "What a pleasure it is to see you again."

Kingsley's eyes burn at the man. "You weren't about to throw my guest out, were you?" he asks lightly.

The maître-d's hands tremble. "Oh no, sir. We were just sorting out her reservation."

"I hope so, because she's with me. It would've been very unfortunate for you if I had to go looking for her outside."

"Sorry, sir. It won't happen again."

"I hope not." Kingsley nods assertively at me to follow him. "Scarlett?"

He offers his hand.

Without a word, I take his strong hand and he pulls me away from the quivering maître-d. Kingsley shoots him a look that makes the man gasp in worry. Kingsley doesn't care.

He leads me to the tearoom, and to a table he must've been waiting for me at.

"Much better," he says when we sit. "I apologize for that man's behavior. That certainly was a one-off. This hotel would normally never accept such snobbery from the staff. I better have a word with the manager."

"I was worried that I was going to have security called on my ass back there," I say, my voice still a high-pitched cheep. "A whole army to haul me out."

"The Heath-Harding name can get you into a lot of places," Kingsley says, leaning forward with a smile. "It can also scare haughty waiters. That can be a lot of fun."

I eye him. He's so self-assured. He's grown up in power and knows how to wield it. It's kind of scary and that turns me on. Of course it bloody does.

"What kind of tea do they have here?" I ask, glancing around the tearoom, trying to divert my thoughts away from what might be hiding under Kingsley's suit. The tearoom is brightly lit by tall windows that look outside. You would think – being in this luxury hotel - that you're in some presidential palace and not in the center of London.

Kingsley hands me a menu. "They serve all kinds of tea here. How about I order for us?"

Looking down at the menu, I feel like it's all written in a foreign language. I don't know any teas at all, except for Earl Grey and English Breakfast, and that's only because I've heard them mentioned in British movies. I'm such a basic bitch. "Yep, that sounds great," I reply quickly. "You order for us."

Thank goodness he's a decisive man ready to take charge.

Kingsley gestures for a waitress.

"My usual," he tells her. She nods. "Same for my guest."

She's really nice. A welcome change to the maître-d.

I may not be a tea drinker, but when you're at the London Grand Hotel, you better drink tea and eat scones. When in Rome and all that.

"I'm happy you made it today," Kingsley says to me when the waitress disappears.

"You're *happy*?"

"I thought you might not show. You were really giving me a sour look last night."

"Well, here I am," I reply. I still don't know what I'm doing here. The temptation of being in close proximity of Kingsley has clearly gotten the better of me.

"It's good to see I've still got a hold on you."

"You do not," I reply quickly. "You definitely don't."

God, this man.

He leans forward conspiratorially. "The other night at the press party suggests otherwise."

"I was drunk," I retort. "And I was pretty shocked by seeing you there. You have no "hold" on me."

I throw up speech mark signs with my hands around the word *hold* just to emphasize my point.

"Well, you seemed pleased to see me," Kingsley continues, unfazed. "I thought you were going to hang around, after all your friends had gone, to chat with me longer."

"I wasn't."

"But now you're here. With me. Alone."

I shake my head. I don't like how he thinks I'll fall at his feet merely because of his charm and good looks. Like he said the other night, I've still got that fiery spark in me, and I'm determined to show it. I've still got some questions that need answering. "Why did you leave me, Kingsley? Why did you run away from Crystal River without a word?"

Kingsley sighs and leans back into his seat as if he's been expecting this question. Good. He should be expecting this. What did he think was going to happen? I'm not gonna just crawl into his bed just because he wants me to and with zero explanation of his behavior.

"It's hard for you to understand," he replies.

Can't he see my blood is boiling?

"Hard for me to understand? Now I'm insulted as well as heartbroken."

"Scarlett..."

"Do you think I'm stupid, Kingsley?"

"No. Certainly not."

"Then why are you treating me like I am? I deserve an explanation for what you did."

Kingsley pauses for a long time. He sits perfectly still, thinking. He eventually speaks. "My father forced me to come back to the UK."

"Your father?"

"Yes, Lord Heath-Harding."

"Come on, Kingsley. Don't give me that *Lord* bullshit."

"Well, he is one."

"And he brought you back here from Crystal River?" I ask. "The big old scary Lord?"

"Yes, he did. Practically against my will."

"What? Like you were some kind of prisoner?"

"It may sound hard to believe it, but my name has a hold over me that sometimes I can't fight against, Scarlett. There are duties I have to carry out."

I want to laugh. We're not living in medieval times. Does he take me for a fool?

"And were you enjoying America?"

Kingsley's blue eyes blaze into mine. "I was enjoying *you*, Scarlett."

"Then why didn't you tell your father so? Why didn't you just say you were going to stay?"

"Because I'm a Heath-Harding, and – as I've said - that family name means something. Responsibilities. Loyalties. I couldn't disrespect the wishes of my father. Despite how much you might mock it, he is a Lord, and his word is power. In both my household and in Parliament. Can't you see? I couldn't go against his wishes."

"And what about your mom?" I ask. "Couldn't you talk to her? Couldn't she do something?"

"She died when I was young," Kingsley says quietly, looking away.

"Oh. I'm so sorry."

That changes things. I imagine Kingsley as a boy without his mother. Alone. Vulnerable.

So different from this six-foot hunk sitting across from me. But maybe that's it. Maybe all of this strength he has is simply his defense from being that little motherless boy again.

"Don't be sorry," he says. "It was a long time ago. I hardly remember her."

I want to get to the bottom of this. I want to understand more about this man sitting opposite me. He's been an enigma in my head for far too long.

"Do you have anyone else? A sibling you can talk to?"

Kingsley nods. "My brother. Duke."

"You two close?"

"Yeah, especially with us having to basically parent each other after mum passed."

"What about your father?"

"Lord Heath-Harding has always... preferred to distance himself. He's always been out of the picture. So Duke and I were left to our own devices."

"I see."

"I think you'll like Duke, although he's a nightmare for any girl."

"Just like his brother," I say. "I guess it runs in the family. And what did he think when you left Crystal River?"

"He wouldn't understand what happened in America."

"I see."

"So, I couldn't stay," Kingsley continues. "But I didn't contact you. I was scared of breaking your heart."

"But my heart did break, Kingsley. I had no closure. I heard *nothing* from you. Do you understand how horrible that was?"

"Yeah, I do now."

"It tore me up."

"I fucked up, Scarlett. I did. I was young and selfish. I thought the pain would be easier for you if I just said nothing at all when I left, but now I know that it was wrong to behave like that. So wrong. I've been thinking about what I did, and I wish I could just turn back time. Every day I've been thinking that. For four years. I want you to know that I've been torn up about it as well all these years. It wasn't just you that's been hurting. I've not been able to get you out of my head since that night in America. No one else has ever compared to you. No one."

"No one?"

"I wouldn't be saying this to anyone else," Kingsley replies, looking directly at me now. My heart thuds in my chest. "I would never let myself be so stripped bare emotionally in front of anyone else. I would never admit my feelings for a girl in front of her. Except for you."

"Kingsley..."

I whisper, but he continues. I want to him to. I want to hear this from him.

"I was a big coward for running away from you like that," Kingsley says, his head bowed. "And for that, I'm so sorry."

I reach forward and hold his hands. His delicate hands. I can see that motherless boy in his eyes.

I know he's telling the truth.

"It's okay, Kingsley."

I'm forgiving him.

I hope he understands how big that is. I hope he understands how much of a shadow his sudden departure left looming over my life and how big of a deal it is for me to forgive the man.

But now he's sitting here, and I do honestly think he's telling the truth. It's hard, but I really do forgive him. I want to move on. I don't want to live under the pain of that teenage heartbreak any longer.

And his earnest groveling certainly helps.

"I forgive you."

He sighs like he's a tangled knot being unfurled. He's affected by this much more than I thought he would be.

"Thank you."

I smile weakly and look away.

"Really," he says. "Thank you."

"It's okay."

"Tell me one thing though, Scarlett," he asks me.

My ears perk up. "What is it?"

"Who was that drunk guy with you at the press party?"

"Who are you talking about?"

"The theater manager guy."

"Oh. You mean Giles?"

Kingsley nods sternly.

And then I realize why he's asking me that question. He's actually jealous of my boss. He might even think we're sleeping together or something. The thought makes me chortle.

Ha.

But Kingsley is not amused.

Oh, how I like him envious like this. All bristling with suspicion. He must hate to think he might not be the only man in my life.

And I'm not prepared to dispel his suspicions.

"Giles is nice. He's my boss."

"Hm."

He's so jealous.

Oh, it's so fun to see him like this.

Our food and teapots arrive. Everything is presented in a gold cage with different layers. Sandwiches at the bottom, followed on the next level by scones with cream and jam, and then various tiny bits of dessert on top. It's exquisite.

"This is proper afternoon tea," I exclaim to Kingsley as I pick up a cup and pour the tea into it. I raise it to my lips. God, it tastes great. I guess drinking tea in the London Grand Hotel makes it even sweeter.

"Yeah, it is."

I'm going to give him a show.

"You like me being here?" I ask sultrily as I remove a scone from the gold cage.

"Oh, yes," Kingsley replies.

I take a knife and smear the scone with jam and then clotted cream until it's covered in it. I seductively bring it to my wet mouth.

Kingsley watches my tongue intensely as I slowly lick the delicious cream off the top of the scone. I love the smolder he gives me, all mixed with jealousy and horniness. I love his obvious longing for my tongue. The cream is cold in my mouth, and I take my time devouring it. I love teasing him like this. I really hope his cock is hard because I'm going to give him nothing but blue balls.

"Don't do this to me, Scarlett."

"Do what?"

I guess my little show works. Kingsley looks very turned on. I feel like he's *aching* to rip my clothes off right here in the middle of the hotel and have his way with me in front of the rest of the guests.

"Thanks for inviting me here," I say as I take another sip

of tea. I'm not going to give into him that easily. "I would never have gone to the London Grand Hotel otherwise."

He seems like he's holding himself back. His animal side has been awakened by my seductive display.

"How long have you been in London?" Kingsley asks.

"Literally a few days."

"Wow. Right, give me your phone number."

"What?"

"Give me your phone number, Scarlett."

Yeah, he's really turned on.

"Why?"

"I'm going to take you out and about. Show you the sights. It's the least I can do."

"You don't have to do that, Kingsley. I don't need a guide."

He laughs. "It's the very least I can do. I feel like I should act as the host now that you're in my home city. After all, I did make that promise to you four years ago in your bedroom that I would show you around if you ever came."

I shrug. Well, this afternoon has certainly ended up very differently from what I imagined.

"Okay then."

* * *

"I'll drive you."

We're standing outside the front door of the London Grand Hotel, on the pavement next to the busy road.

"It's okay, Kingsley. I can make my own way home."

He nods towards his parked Aston Martin. "Come on, I'll drive you to wherever you want to go."

I smile coyly. "I prefer to walk. I like to see London on foot. Explore it a little."

Kingsley shakes his head. Without saying a word, he reaches forward and slowly traces his finger around my chin. Dancing the tip of it on my lip. I have the sudden temptation to open my mouth to suck it. When he lifts his finger away, I can taste cinnamon. It's the same taste as his aftershave. It makes me think of kissing that rough stubble of his.

"I'll never understand you, Scarlett," Kingsley eventually says.

"Really?"

"You've been a total mystery to me since I first saw you walking around Crystal River High with the complete works of Shakespeare under your arm. Maybe that's why I can't resist you."

"You can't resist me?"

"I'll like to do something like this again. Show you around London. How does that sound?"

I giggle. "I'm not completely against that idea."

He leans down and whispers into my ear. "Maybe you can do another show for me like you just did in there. You know, with the cream."

Today has been really nice. He's a good date, I'll give him that.

"If you're lucky," I whisper back.

Kingsley's eyes light up. He likes that.

"I'll message you," he says.

Oh, I know I'm going to be dreaming about this day for a long time.

28

KINGSLEY

I AM late for the theater. I quickly pull up in my Aston Martin and try to rush inside. There are a lot of fans waiting for me outside stage door though, and – like a good celebrity - I can't let them down, so I stay and take selfies with each of them. Smile and talk. I really make sure I speak to every single person waiting for me before I enter the theater. These are the people who truly matter to my career, not the critics or the producers. My real audience.

I sign myself in before sprinting through the narrow hallways towards my dressing room.

I don't make it there before Penelope emerges from her own room, deliberately blocking me from going any further. She's been lying in ambush for me.

The serious look on her face means she wants to talk.

Fucking hell.

She's sprung out of nowhere.

"Who is she?" the woman asks.

I narrow my eyes at my co-star.

"What?"

"The girl. Who is she?"

"I don't know what you're talking about," I reply.

Penelope rolls her eyes, exasperated, and angrily crosses her arms. "The girl at the London Grand Hotel? Who is she? I had a friend who was there today, and they saw you. With a girl."

"Oh. Right."

If Penelope's eyebrow could be raised up any further, then she'll break her perfectly smooth forehead. "Apparently she's got an American accent," she mutters.

I try to push past her, but she's really standing in my way, and I don't want to hurt her, so I stand still.

"I don't have time for this, Penelope. I need to get ready. I'm already so late."

"Who is she, King?"

Wow. She really is furious. I sleep with a girl one time, and she acts like we're a married couple.

Jesus.

"She is a friend."

I want to throw her off the scent. I can't deal with a furious Penelope during tonight's performance. I still have to act with the woman, for goodness' sake.

"Really? She's a *friend?* Apparently, she was practically licking the cream from around your mouth. That's some friend you've got there."

"Fucking hell."

"Just tell me, King. What were you doing with her?"

"Now, look here Penelope. I would prefer it if you didn't follow me around."

"My friend saw you. They told me. I had nothing to do with it."

"You sure they weren't there on your orders?"

"King..."

I raise my hand and interrupt her. "You and I are not in a relationship, Penelope. We're colleagues on a stage. You have no right to my personal life. You got that? Don't send any more of your lackeys to follow me, okay?"

I shuffle past her and head into my dressing room. I can hear Penelope's irritated huffs until I shut the door.

My publicist, Ben, is waiting for me in my dressing room. Standing in the middle of the room with a sour look on his face.

"Great," I say. "Today seems to be the day everyone wants to spring out and surprise me."

Ben scoffs. "You know why I'm here, King."

"Shoot."

Even though I am annoyed, I do have time for Ben. I shouldn't be pissed off at him; he's the rock in my career. Always pointing me in the right direction. Serious and stern, he's one I can steadfastly rely on to always make the best decisions for me.

Even if he can be so fucking insistent with making me do things I don't want to do.

"You need to do some press, King. You may be the talk of the town right now, deservedly so, but you can't avoid interviews," he says. "You need them to get on the next rung of the ladder."

"Sure," I reply. "I'll do some."

"Good lad."

But the last thing I want to think of right now is appeasing some hungry journalist. All I'm thinking of is Scarlett Hart and her fiery red hair.

29

SCARLETT

India hates me. I can tell. She's hated me from the minute Giles paired us up together on press night. And tonight, she spends the entire show sitting across the auditorium from me sending death stares in my direction.

Yep, she really flipping hates me.

Which is why, when I arrive home to the flat, I carelessly throw my bag on the floor by the front door and immediately slump into the welcoming embrace of the sofa. I'm sick and tired.

"You alright?" Grace asks me from the other side of the couch. She's all wrapped up in a comfy blanket. She's wearing bright pink pajamas, which is something I would never expect Grace to wear. But if there's one thing I've learned by living with her, it's that you should expect the unexpected from that woman.

On the TV is a very gory true crime documentary. Another one that's all about some lone woman walking home late at night being murdered by some creepy-ass dude with mommy issues.

Another thing I've come to know about Grace is that she watches a lot of those.

"Hard day at work," I sigh, rubbing my forehead. "That's all."

At least I have tomorrow off from work. It'll be Sunday. No theater shows on Sunday.

"What's wrong?"

"I'm already on my final warning, and I also think everyone I work with hates me."

"Well, I love you," Grace replies before she mutes the TV. "I'm sure that counts for something, yeah? How about some wine? Will that help? A little bit of liquid medicine?"

She doesn't have to ask me twice.

"Absolutely."

Grace collects a very nice bottle of Australian Chardonnay from the fridge with two glasses, and we practically down it.

"And let's order pizza," Grace suggests, pulling out her phone to order from an app. "I know a really cool Italian place around the corner from here. I'm sure a good wood-fired pizza will help you recover from a bad day at work."

"I think you're right."

When it arrives, we devour the pizza very much like the wine. It really does help me forget the work shift. And India. And my crappy manager.

"You should visit me at my work," Grace says, rubbing her full belly contentedly.

"The Jack the Ripper tour, right?"

"I think you'll like it. Lots of murder."

"Sounds right up your street," I reply, nodding at the muted crime documentary still playing on the TV. "No wonder you work there. Yeah, I think I will take you up on your offer someday. I'll like to get to know a bit more about the seedy parts of London."

My phone beeps on the table next to the remains of the pizza. I reach over to pick it up.

Kingsley.

Grace leans forward.

"Who is it?" she asks, obviously seeing my face drop.

Just the sight of that man's name makes my stomach turn. It's like he has a permanent hold over me and I cannot escape.

I don't even know if I *want* to escape.

HELLO MISS PRIDE AND PREJUDICE.

I want to take you out tomorrow night.

I will be outside yours at 6.

Wear something nice.

THE AUDACITY of Kingsley to just assume I'm free tomorrow and to also assume I won't say no. It's very annoying, but also very masculine. Strong. Powerful. Cheeky.

And – fucking hell - it turns me on.

30

SCARLETT

Kingsley is exactly on time.

I watch from the top window of Grace's flat as I see his Aston Martin park next to the fish and chip shop. A very weird combination of greasy food and a flashy car.

I see the driver's door open, and all six feet something of Kingsley Heath-Harding steps out like a knight dismounting a horse.

My heart flutters.

He's dressed in a sharp suit.

I bite my lip and look down at what I'm wearing. I followed what he said and decided on the nicest dress I've brought from America. Well, I hope it isn't too much, but at least I know I look good in it.

I'm not wearing the dress for him. I promised myself a long time ago that I would never wear a dress for a guy unless it's a white one at an altar and I'm hearing the words *I do*.

I head downstairs and open the door before Kingsley gets the chance to buzz.

His eyes scan me up and down before he speaks. Admiring me. Oh, I'm glad I'm wearing this dress tonight. I know what he's thinking. He's mentally stripping me, and I like it.

"Hello, Scarlett."

That voice. That accent.

Under my dress, I feel my nipples harden.

"Kingsley."

"Call me King."

"Nope. Never gonna happen, so you better just drop it."

He smiles, making my insides melt.

"Can I come inside?"

I look back into the flat nervously. The last thing I want is for Kingsley to be standing in my bedroom. I don't know what'll happen if he did.

Also, it's a bit of a mess. Grace and I were too lazy this morning to clean up the pizza scraps. Can't have this guy who looks like he's stepped out of a Disney film come snooping around my pigsty.

"Not in a million years, Kingsley."

"Aw, damn. I would very much like to see your bed."

"Well, you can't."

"It'll be even better to see you naked in it."

"*Kingsley.*"

He winks. "Oh, you love it, babe."

"So, where are you taking me tonight?" I ask demurely.

"It's a surprise." He offers his arm. "Follow me."

As I'm heading away from the flat, I spot Rick standing in the window of the fish and chip shop downstairs. He's glaring at us with his arms crossed. Glaring at Kingsley. It takes me a moment to realize the Cockney is just being super protective of me with this strange man. I give Rick a thumbs up and he instantly smiles, content. It's cute how Rick really is looking out for us.

Kingsley guides me to his car, opening the door like a proper gentleman.

"Very chivalrous," I remark.

"I do come from good breeding, Scarlett."

Oh, he most certainly does.

We sit in the car, and he powers up the ignition.

It's so plush inside. I've never sat in a more luxurious car. I feel like a movie star or a princess. I feel like a million bucks.

Kingsley effortlessly drives us away from my flat and into the center of London. The lights of the city quickly flash by.

"Come on, tell me," I ask him. "Where are we going?"

Kingsley doesn't take his cool eyes off the road. "It's a surprise."

"Alright then. Keep your secrets," I say. "But tell me one thing. How did you know my address?"

Both Grace and I had been wondering about that all day. His message to me didn't ask me where I lived, and I had never told the man. How did he know where to find me?

Kingsley turns to me and winks cheekily. "Being the son of a billionaire lord does have its privileges," he says.

"Oh. Right. I forgot you had MI6 at your beck and call."

"You know, I did do a background check on you," he tells me cheekily.

My eyes widen. "You did?"

"Yep."

"And what did you find?"

I'm so curious.

"Well, I have to take precautions, given my family name. Can't be associated with a criminal. You're clean."

"Great."

"But there is one issue with you that was flagged up."

"What?" I ask.

Kingsley coyly smiles again. "Your amazing ass. The issue is that it might make me do things I'll find difficult to resist."

I blush.

"Shut up, Kingsley."

"We're here," he says, pulling the car to a stop in front of a tall building. I look up at it from the window.

"The British Library?"

"Yep," Kingsley replies.

I honestly don't know what's going on, but Kingsley opens my side door and brings me inside the dark building.

It's shut. It's long after it's closed to visitors, but Kingsley takes me to a side entrance where a security guard nods at him and lets him through.

We step into the main foyer of the British Library.

At the top of the stairs, a man is waiting for us. He claps his hands together when he sees us.

"Hello, Kingsley," the man says.

"This is Trevor," Kingsley says to me, introducing the man. "He's a curator of the collection here."

Trevor bounces down the stairs and gives me a handshake.

"Pleasure to meet you, Scarlett. Kingsley has told me a lot about you."

"What has he said?" I ask. "Nothing bad, I hope."

"Oh, he told me your interests."

"My interests?"

Kingsley nudges me playfully on the arm. "You'll see," he says. "Trevor has kindly agreed to stay behind tonight to give us a private tour of the collection here. I'd rather see all this without a crowd."

"Exactly," Trevor agrees. "It's the best way to see it. Come with me."

He turns and leads us up the staircase to another room. I mouth to Kingsley.

What is going on?

He merely raises his finger to his lips and hushes me. With his other hand, he grabs mine and pulls me close. I rub up against his firm muscles and continue up the stairs.

The boy is good at surprises, I must say. My heart is racing. I don't know what he has in store for me.

We enter a small, dark room.

"This part of the Library is usually shut off from the public," Trevor exclaims. "Very valuable items are housed here that we don't often exhibit. You are a very lucky lady to be seeing these, Scarlett."

We pass by cases with the most amazing antiques. I can't help myself but look inside.

"Is that a First Folio of Shakespeare?" I ask as we walk by a case housing a big, thick book. "No *freaking* way."

"That's not even the best bit," Kingsley says.

"You know, when Kingsley told me why he wanted to come here tonight, I was pretty perplexed," Trevor explains as he guides us further into the dark room. "It's usually impossible to show anyone this, let alone actually allow them to touch it. But when he explained about you, I just had to give you a private tour."

He takes us to a table set up just for us. There's a single book resting on top.

"There we are," Kingsley says.

"What is it?"

He pushes me towards it, and I read the handwritten title on the book.

I gasp.

"Is this what I think it is?"

"Yes," Kingsley says. "It's Jane Austen's handwritten first draft of Pride and Prejudice."

I have no words. Trevor hands me a pair of gloves to put on so I don't damage the pages.

And then I actually get to *freaking* touch the book. The same pages Jane Austen herself wrote on. My whole arms shake with trepidation as I slowly work my way through the pages, reading over her neat handwriting.

I literally don't make a sound. I can't believe it.

Trevor gives me a very informed commentary about it. About certain words she uses. About how the paper was made and how she would've written back in that time.

My mouth hangs agape the entire session.

"How did you manage to do all this?" I ask Kingsley when Trevor leaves us to spend time alone with the book.

His blue eyes sparkle under the dim lights. "You know, Scarlett, being the son of a billionaire lord really does have its privileges."

"You're impossible," I reply.

"So. This is my apology for what happened four years ago," he says quietly.

"It's really some apology. You never forgot I'm into Jane Austen?"

"Never."

"Wow."

"And just you wait till you see where we're going next."

31

KINGSLEY

IN THE CAR, Scarlett holds my hand all the way to the club. She doesn't let go once. Her finger entwines with mine like she can't get enough of me. It makes my cock stiff.

I think it's pretty fair to say that the whole *Jane Austen manuscript* thing was a roaring success.

Feeling her hand in mine, I'm pretty proud of my idea of taking the girl on a private tour of the British Library. Seeing her gorgeous face light up when she spotted the manuscript on the table and the way her fuckable lips softly parted as she scanned the handwriting, deep in thought, brought me so much joy.

And has made me incredibly horny.

It's been pretty hard to hide my near-permanent erection.

I pull my car up outside the club in the middle of Mayfair, an extravagant part of central London not far from the London Grand Hotel.

The Palace is one of the most exclusive spots in all of

Mayfair, and that's saying something. Scarlett deserves nothing less from a night out with me. To have even a chance to get into the club, you have to either wait in line for hours to potentially get turned away, or you have to have the right powerful connections.

Of course, I have the latter.

"Mr. Heath-Harding," the bouncer greets me formally at the door, lifting the velvet rope to let Scarlett and I skip the queue.

The girl on my arm gasps as we enter. She must've heard about the Palace before. She must know how exclusive it is.

I like being able to show this elite side of London to her. I like treating her like a queen. I want Scarlett to experience what it might be like to be my girl for a night. A Heath-Harding girl.

I usher her to my regular booth in the far back corner of the club, past the dance floor.

A long and illuminated bar runs along one wall. There are sparkling candles and immense bottles of Russian vodka decorating the bar. Rows of fancy glasses line the walls. Smiling waitresses with plunging cleavages pouring shots for rich businessmen and celebrities. I think I spot a member of the hottest boy band on the planet right now. He's surrounded by adoring girls with stars in their eyes.

This is my world, and Scarlett is getting to experience it tonight.

"This is *amazing*," the American girl says to me, shaking her head in disbelief at the surroundings of the club as we hover next to my booth.

"Welcome to my kingdom," I reply.

I watch her take in the famous nightclub. "There's just so many pretty people here," she remarks. "So many people I've seen on the screen or in a music video or on Instagram."

I lean in over her shoulder so that I can whisper in her ear.

"You're the prettiest person here," I say. "My eyes are only on you."

"Only on me?"

"Well, and let's not forget your amazing ass."

I reach down to grab her tempting booty, but before my hand can get a piece of it, Scarlett playfully flicks me away.

"Don't think that just because you show a gal an original first draft of Pride and Prejudice and then you take her to a fancy club that you're free to spank her ass, Kingsley."

"Okay, so what will it take, then?"

She smirks up at me. That fiery spark of hers fucking turns me on so much.

"Well, a nice glass of champagne would be a good start."

"Stay here," I growl, pointing at the booth before quickly turning around and heading for the bar.

I feel Scarlett's eyes on my own ass as I saunter away. The girl is naughty.

I know the bartender working tonight; he's served me plenty of times. He hands over the glass of champagne and a glass of Scotch for me.

I walk back to my booth to see Scarlett still standing at the edge of it.

And she's speaking to a strange man.

I immediately size him up. He's about the same height as me, but definitely skinnier. Fake tan. A guy that's no more than a four out of ten, but who's self-deluded enough to think he's six points higher. A guy who probably sends out at least five unsolicited dick pics a day to girls who definitely don't want them.

To be honest, I don't care what he looks like or what his personality is. I don't care about him at all.

But what I do care about him is the fact that he has his

arms around Scarlett's waist, and she's trying to squirm to get out.

What. The. Fuck.

Even with the music, I overhear what he's saying to her.

"Come on, just one dance, baby girl. Why don't you wanna dance with me? I'll give you a good time."

"I said no," Scarlett bluntly replies, still attempting to push his wandering hand away before it reaches her breast.

That's it.

I've seen enough.

This shithead is about to get what's coming to him.

I reckon Scarlett has the balls to fight him off, but it's my time to step in. Deal with this.

I place the two drinks on a nearby ledge and approach Scarlett and the man from behind.

I only say one word.

"Scarlett."

It isn't a question. It's a direct challenge to this asshole with his fucking hands around my girl. It's a warning to back the fuck off right fucking now.

They both turn to look at me. The man bares his teeth, sensing a threat. Scarlett's face is full of relief at seeing me. Her grateful expression makes me feel even more protective over her.

"Who's this prick?" the man asks Scarlett, nodding towards me.

"Let her go."

I don't shout. I don't swear. My low voice is enough.

I want this man to know that I mean danger. The real kind. I want this man to know that no one messes with my girl.

"You're a joker," the asshole replies. He turns to a group of men standing nearby. I realize they must be his friends. They haven't said anything yet, they're just staring at me. They can sense my bubbling anger and clearly don't want to get involved. "He's a joker, right, lads?"

"Leave him," one of the asshole's friends quietly suggests. "Let's just go, mate."

"Oh, don't worry," asshole man replies. "I can take this prick on. He's nothing to me."

I clench my fist slowly.

I am calm. I am confident. Everything is clear to me. I see Scarlett's eyes dart down to my fists. She looks worried, but not for me.

She's worried for the asshole.

I think she already suspects my physical power.

"I don't want to do this, *mate,*" I say. Leisurely, so that the words can get through this bloke's thick skull. "But I will have to if you don't let go of her in the next three seconds."

The asshole scoffs.

That's a mistake.

"Piss off," he replies.

Another mistake.

"Two seconds," I warn.

"I'll floor ya."

So. *He's threatening me now?*

"One second. Let go of her."

"That's it," the man says. "You're gonna get it."

That's his last mistake.

It all happens so suddenly. The man pulls back his arm.

Scarlett screams.

The asshole takes a swing at me. I duck easily enough. His arm flies way over my head.

Then I launch a fist at the asshole's jaw. He doesn't see it coming at all.

It's a perfect punch. My hand hits his chin square-on. I feel bone crunching. Not my bone.

And then the man collapses. Knocked out in one single punch. He lies on the dance floor, unconscious.

My unqualified diagnosis is that he's probably going to have to spend a few weeks at the hospital. Maybe his jaw won't ever be the same again. A simple lesson learned hard.

Don't mess with another man's girl, especially if that guy is a Heath-Harding.

The man's friends all look on in frozen terror. They can't believe what's happened. The speed at which I've knocked their mate out.

Then security arrives. Two bouncers I know.

I turn to them.

"We won't be needing you chaps," I say before firmly taking Scarlett by the hand out of the club.

The whole time we spend navigating through the busy dance floor, Scarlett just looks up at me, unblinking. She looks nowhere else. I understand that expression on her face.

Awe.

Of me.

And, I have to say, I fucking *love* it.

No one touches my girl. Except for me.

32

SCARLETT

"Holy shit," I exclaim, sitting back in Kingsley's plush Aston Martin. "You actually *punched* a guy!"

I throw my head back and loudly laugh at the ridiculousness of it all.

"You knocked him out in one go! He was just *lying* there like a lump, thanks to you."

Kingsley drives the car with deadly seriousness. Unlike me, he is definitely not laughing at what just happened. His face is solid. Stern.

He's so sexy when he's pissed. It's just like the way he said my name back in the club when he spotted that guy's arm around my waist. So dark and brooding. So *possessive*.

I really had thought in the club that Kingsley would forget all about me. I'm not blind; I saw how the other girls in the place admired Kingsley as he entered. I can't blame them. I was envious of all the rich and beautiful people in there and how the man sitting next to me fitted in with them so easily. I do not belong in a Mayfair club like the Palace;

I'm just your typical girl next door from small town America.

I really thought Kingsley would leave me alone in the booth. But then he came back for me, and that protective gleam in his eyes told me everything I needed to know. This man sitting next to me is willing to *fight* for me.

Kingsley takes his gleaming eyes off the road to look at me.

"Are you okay?" he asks, his voice low and rumbling like thunder. "Are you hurt?"

"I'm fine," I reply. Kingsley checks me out carefully from his seat like he doesn't believe me with all the protectiveness of a lion over his herd. Like I'm one of those precious, fragile items stored in the British Library. "I'm better than fine. I just witnessed you completely destroy that guy."

"So, you're okay?"

"Kingsley, I just had a front-row seat of you doing a one-punch knockout on an asshole. Of course I'm okay. This has been one of the best nights ever."

"I didn't know you like violence," he says.

"Well, you don't know that much about me, then," I reply. Kingsley turns from me and changes gear. I can tell he's thinking of me. I'm not dumb; I can see the outline of his erection in his pants. My mouth waters at the sight of it.

Adrenaline is pulsing through my veins, and so is my horniness. I know, in my bath later this week, that I'm going to be thinking back on tonight and Kingsley's immediate violent reaction to my honor being threatened. I know that I won't be able to not touch myself thinking of the serious way Kingsley looks at me now and how he calmly changes gear with skill.

The Aston Martin roars across London. Kingsley is

speeding, but he clearly doesn't care. He's probably still buzzing from that interaction as well.

We speed down a road next to the Thames until I can see Tower Bridge rise up ahead of us.

"Where are we going now?" I ask.

"Back to mine," Kingsley growls, his hands caressing the steering wheel through the narrow streets of London.

I don't object to this new destination.

He spins us into an underground parking lot right next to Tower Bridge. This must be the building where he lives.

Kingsley doesn't say anything as he parks the car and opens the door for me, taking me to a private elevator that soars above the city to a penthouse apartment at the very top of the building.

"This is your place?" I ask as we step into the living room. I seem to be finding myself completely disarmed by every new thing Kingsley shows me tonight. It's hard not to when he's presenting such an upper-class world to me.

He leads such a cool and interesting life.

Do I even fit into it?

Kingsley's place has floor-to-ceiling windows with a magnificent close-up view of Tower Bridge and the river. Big Ben and the Houses of Parliament sparkle in the distance. The city is all around us. It's like a postcard view of London.

It must be a very *expensive* view of London.

"Yep, this is mine," Kingsley replies. "Make yourself at home. You want a drink?"

"Yes please," I say as I stare out over the Thames, mouth open in dazzlement. "Make it strong. Very strong."

Kingsley fetches me a Scotch with a drop of water. I would normally refuse a drink *this* strong, but right now I need it. Tonight has been a hell of a crazy night.

"You sure you're okay?" Kingsley asks, continuing to scan my body carefully.

"Stop saying that," I reply, taking a seat on one of Kingsley's luxurious pure-white chairs. "I am fine. The man only managed to just put his arm around me and nothing more, thanks to you."

He sits down next to me. "Good."

"You know, it was kinda sexy how you came to my rescue," I say, taking a long sip of the lovely Scotch. "Kinda like a knight in shining armor. My very own knight."

"And that makes you a damsel-in-distress, right?"

"I think of myself more as a free-spirited independent kick-ass princess who *sometimes* requires the services of a handsome knight."

Kingsley puts his arm around me and spreads his legs out like a dominant tiger. He undoes his tie and top button, granting me a precious glimpse of his firm, tanned chest. I can watch his muscular body move in his tight clothes all night, but I really need to take my eyes off his hot body. Kingsley's own gaze slips down to my dress, resting on my cleavage. There's a sudden rush of heat through my body.

"So now you've changed your tune about me?" Kingsley asks. "I'm not just a dick who broke your heart?"

"Well, we'll still have to see about that."

"Because I can promise you, I won't ever break your heart again."

I put my empty glass of Scotch down on the table and stare at the man. Now it's my turn to be serious.

"Don't make promises you can't keep, Kingsley. They're the ones that really can ruin everyone involved."

"Oh, I can promise this one," he replies coolly.

"You'll excuse me if I don't allow myself to get hurt again."

"You don't need to close yourself off to me," Kingsley

whispers. "I will do anything for you. I will fight a whole army of assholes to make sure no man ever touches you again. I can promise you that."

"Still on the knight in shining armor thing, are you?"

"If I'm a knight, then that makes you my queen. A true knight will fight to the death for his queen."

He reaches behind my neck and gently pulls my head towards him.

Like when he told me he was taking me to his apartment, I don't object.

The way he looks at me now. It beats even the possessive look he gave me in the club. I want this moment to last forever.

The kiss, when our lips finally touch, is long and strong. Something we've both been waiting to do for a long time.

He devours me, kissing me as I've never been kissed before. Slowly. His spare hand dances around the edge of my dress, feeling my smooth legs. Making my whole body shiver. My breasts swell. My clit aches to be touched. I spread my hand on his hot chest. His heartbeat vibrates against my fingers as I suck on his tongue. This is even better than the memories of that night in high school.

And that's when I know that I can no longer keep my heart closed off from this man. I've lost all control. He has me now.

I savor his mouth. His tenderness as his fingers run through my hair.

I wrap my leg over him and rest my weight on his knees so that I'm straddling him. We continue to kiss deeply as I begin to rub myself over his crotch. We're both still fully clothed. Kingsley whimpers in my mouth as I feel his cock stiffen under his pants. He's so damn thick, and it turns me on so much. My hands run down the front of his suit, and I feel his firm chest muscles. The man is solid and strong. A shudder runs through my pussy as I start to hump him faster and deeper. Any longer and we'll both be orgasming without either of our genitals touching...

Kingsley moans again. I start to pant.

But I know this moment can't last forever.

Before I launch into a mouth-watering orgasm and before Kingsley's hard cock explodes, I lift myself up and away from his lap. My whole body screams at me not to, but I know I must.

Our lips part.

The moment ends and clarity returns.

I remember crying in the cubicle at Crystal River High when I found out he'd gone back to London. I remember those nights of heartbreak.

"I'm drunk," I say, almost as an excuse.

It's true. I can't trust my instincts right now. We can't rush into anything.

Kingsley pauses for a long time. I can't read what he's thinking. "Did you want to do that?" he asks quietly.

I don't answer that question. I don't feel like I can. I don't know where my head - or my heart - is at right now. I certainly can't be doing something reckless at midnight just because my body is full of adrenaline and endorphins.

"I think I need to go to bed," I say.

Kingsley nods. "You can have my room. I'll sleep on the sofa."

I like how he doesn't push me into doing anything.

I don't know what I'll do if he does. Probably something I will regret. Or something I will enjoy.

What if he took me to bed and then lost interest? Would it all just be a repeat of four years ago? I couldn't have that again.

He takes me into his room. His bed is so well-made and tight that I'm scared of ruining it by sleeping in it.

We barely speak to each other as I get ready for sleep. There's a quiet tension between us. Something has been broken by that kiss. A point of no return. But neither of us is ready to pursue its consequences just yet.

We both need time to process what just happened. Well, I certainly do.

Kingsley is all respectful. A gentleman.

"Goodnight, Scarlett."

"Tonight was fun," I say.

"It was."

"I would like to do it again."

"Me too."

He turns to leave the room, but I skip across to him and pull him back around.

This time it's me kissing him. Another long kiss.

I just want to know how his lips feel like again.

"We're both drunk," he tells me when our faces part. "I want to experience you sober."

And then he's leaving the room, and I spend all night debating whether to find him on the sofa.

But, in the end, I don't.

I fall asleep to the sound of his voice repeating over and over in my head.

I want to experience you sober.

I WAS COMING FOR THEM.

I followed them from the British Library all the way to the club. It was harder than I anticipated. Kingsley Heath-Harding is a very fast driver. I guess that is consistent with his bad boy persona. Mr. Playboy with the fast fancy cars.

I was envious of his lifestyle. Of course I was. The man was everything I wanted to be. Rich, talented, charismatic, and - of course - incredibly good-looking. A hit with the ladies.

And the lady that was currently hanging off his suave arm was Scarlett Hart.

I managed to trail behind them all the way across town to Mayfair. To the Palace. That super elite shithole.

"Fuck," I muttered when they pulled up outside the nightclub.

It may have been easy for someone like Kingsley Heath-Harding, with his charm and notoriety, to worm his way inside the famous club, but it certainly wasn't easy for someone like me.

I decided to risk it, confidently making my way to the front of the queue as Scarlett and Kingsley disappeared inside. I handed a thick roll of pound notes to the bouncer, praying to God it would work.

The bouncer glances me up and down.

With a grunt, he accepted my bribe.

Money. Of course. Human beings are so predictable. It cost me a lot, though. Money I couldn't afford to throw away so frivolously. But I needed to follow them.

I sneaked through the door inside the club.

I stayed in the dark corners, searching the crowded room for the couple.

I couldn't have one of them recognizing me.

I wanted to see the two love birds in action, and I was not disappointed.

I watched them deep in flirty conversation. Kingsley's hands reaching greedily for Scarlett's ass. I watched as Kingsley dodged the fist of some guy bothering Scarlett before launching a perfect blow of his own. I watched them both leave the club hand-in-hand like victors of some great battle, Scarlett beaming up at Kingsley like he was her savior.

Ugh.

Disgusting.

How dare they enjoy themselves? How dare they think they are on top of the world?

I should've been in that position, not them.

I promised to myself right there that I would make them truly understand what it is like to hurt. To feel pain.

Kingsley and Scarlett, I thought to myself, I am coming for you.

33

SCARLETT

I WAKE up thinking that last night was just a dream, but when I open my eyes and look down at Tower Bridge like it's a miniature model below Kingsley's penthouse, I know that last night was as real as they come.

I'd felt hornier than I've ever had before as I lay in Kingsley's bed last night. My clit had throbbed with longing all night and my pussy clenched with need until the early morning. But I still resisted the desire to get out of Kingsley's bed and jump on his dick in the other room. I'm sure he wouldn't protest if I had, and that made everything ten times worse as I lay there in his sheet bathed in his manly scent. I've never wanted anyone more, but did that mean I was just gonna open my legs up and let him have me? No way. But it didn't stop me last night from slowly reaching down under the bedsheets to feel myself. I stroked my wet pussy, thinking of Kingsley as his bedsheets wrapped tight around me. Thinking of him licking his tongue up along my inner thigh and over my clit. I made myself finish thinking of how he'd punched a guy for me in that club and how he was willing to get punched himself to defend my honor like I was some kind of medieval princess. I made my whole body shudder, reminiscing about how he'd watched my mouth the other day at the London Grand Hotel lick that clotted cream off the scone.

The most real thing that happened last night was the taste of Kingsley's lips on mine. I can still taste his cinnamon as I stumble out of his bed.

And then the realization hits me.

I'm the one now in his bedroom.

I know I really shouldn't, but - yeah - I'm gonna snoop around. Look, I'm not going to go anywhere that seems too private.

But it seems like I don't even have to worry about that. I find absolutely nothing incriminating in his bedroom. Just rows of his beautiful, tailored suits hanging in his wardrobe and stacks of half-read plays by his bed.

No signs of women.

No discarded panties lying around. No hidden trophies of his sexual conquests. Nothing juicy.

It would be kinda fun to find evidence of Kingsley's naughty side, but if he has one, then he's smart enough to keep it concealed.

Disappointed, I put on one of his hoodies. It's got the name of the posh fancy boarding school he went to written in large block letters over it. Apparently, he was on the rugby team. *Sexy*. I can imagine him rolling in the dirt, tackling other boys. Getting rough. Getting a black eye. Using all his muscles and strength to carry the ball down the field.

My head thuds from the drinks last night. I head out of the bedroom in search of the kitchen and a glass of water or, even better yet, orange juice and bacon.

I notice Kingsley is still fast asleep on the sofa when I

tiptoe through the living room, dressed only in his oversized hoodie and my panties.

I wonder if he'll find me cute wearing his clothes if he wakes up, seeing my ass bounce across the room.

I stagger into the kitchen.

There's someone in there, an older lady.

The first thing I observe about her is her amazing posture. She moves gracefully. She reminds me of a really cool witch or something. Like Professor McGonagall from Harry Potter.

She turns as I enter. I freeze.

Who is she?

"You must be Scarlett," the woman says with a wink. She's standing in the middle of the kitchen. There are pans and food orderly placed on the counter. She's clearly been prepping to make food. "I was wondering when I would meet you. Kingsley's kept you hidden from me for far too long."

"Um, hi," I reply. I suddenly feel so self-conscious wearing basically nothing, but the woman doesn't seem to care. She continues to glide around the kitchen, opening cupboards and the fridge.

"I assume from your reaction to me that Kingsley has not spoken about me at all," she says with her awesomely sharp English accent as she takes out a bottle of olive oil and places it by the hob. She sighs. "I suspected as much from him. I'm Camilla. Lovely to meet you."

"Oh, he has mentioned you," I splutter. "Nice to meet you."

"Lots of scary stories, I guess?"

"No. Definitely not."

Camilla's lips form into a slight smile. "Hm. You're just being polite. Please sit, I'm making breakfast."

"You don't have to do that," I protest.

She waves my concern away. Every movement of hers is precise and direct, like she's the calmest person on the planet. She really is so cool.

"You two obviously had a big night. Let me make you something little to eat." Camilla gestures into the living room where Kingsley must be still asleep. "He's being a bad host not feeding his guest. Let me make it up for him."

"Well, thank you."

"Would you like some water?"

"Yes please."

As Camilla hands me a glass, the kitchen door opens and Kingsley marches in, still very much bleary-eyed. He's clearly just woken up and is looking worse for wear. His curly hair is even more tousled than usual.

"Oh. Camilla." He seems irritated by her presence. "What are you doing here?"

The woman is unfazed by his loud entrance. "Nice to see you as well, Kingsley. Nice to see you've still got those good manners I spent years instilling in you. You've not offered to get your guest her breakfast. The poor thing is positively starving."

I snort with laughter. Kingsley glares at me. Camilla smirks in her ice-cold British way.

"What are you doing here, Camilla?"

She raises an eyebrow. "Can't a nanny see the boy she raised?"

"For the hundredth time, you're not my nanny."

"If you insist. I'm making breakfast. Please sit with Scarlett."

"Oh, right," Kingsley says. "Camilla, this is Scarlett. Scarlett, this is Camilla. Not my nanny."

"We've already met, Kingsley," Camilla replies. "You're late and totally useless."

I giggle again. I really, really like her. And I especially

like the way she can completely disarm this hunk with just a withering glance.

"Right," Kingsley says before taking a seat at the table next to me.

"Hi," I say to him.

He rubs his hungover eyes and smiles at me. "Hello, Scarlett."

His eyes wander over the hoodie I'm wearing with a thirst. See, he does find me cute.

I bite my lip and try to hold back from swooning.

"Like what you see?" I ask.

"It'll be nicer if you took that hoodie off," he whispers so that Camilla can't hear.

Kingsley's phone then rings. He picks it up and starts to head out of the room.

"Sorry, I have to take this," he says. "It's my acting agent in America."

When he leaves, Camilla glides over to me.

"He likes you, you know," she says.

I shake my head. "I don't know about that."

"Trust me, Scarlett. I raised that boy. I know these things as much as a mother does."

"You think so?"

"I know all about America. I was there. This isn't some momentary thing he has for you. He is apologetic about what happened."

It's like she can read my mind.

"It is... complicated," I reply, hesitant.

"Kingsley's always worn his heart on his sleeve," Camilla replies with a nod. "He's an *actor*, for goodness' sake. He's brimming with emotions, unlike his brother. They're complete opposites. Duke's quieter. More... brooding. Trust me when I say that I know for a certainty that Kingsley likes you. A lot."

"Well, thanks."

She points a finger at me. "But don't you dare tell him I told you so. He thinks I can't see these things, that I don't know what's going on in his head, but to me, he's easier to read than a book."

Kingsley returns, having just hung up from his phone call. He takes his seat next to me and we wait patiently for Camilla to finish making breakfast.

It's a full English.

"My favorite," Kingsley tells me. "Camilla is the best undiscovered chef in the country."

"Stop it, you," she says before giving him a peck on the cheek. Kingsley blushes.

I love their relationship. I love her already.

"This is so good," I say to Camilla with my mouth full of sausages and bacon.

"Good."

We don't speak much as we eat. When we finish, I offer to wash up.

"How long have you been working for the Heath-Hardings?" I ask her.

Camilla smiles at me. "A long time, Scarlett. A very long time."

"She's been annoying me for years," Kingsley interrupts.

"I'm pretty sure it's the other way around," Camilla retorts. "Those two boys were quite the handful."

"I bet," I say. "What were you up to before you were with the Heath-Hardings?"

"Oh, I've lived many lives," Camilla says, smirking coyly. "I've got a few stories that I won't bore you two now by retelling."

"Please do," I reply. "I would love to hear them."

"Maybe someday," Kingsley says.

Camilla continues to smile at me. "Well, I have to head

off," she says, obviously darting away to give Kingsley and me time together. "Please call me, Kingsley. Or visit. And you're welcome anytime, Scarlett. You don't even need to come with this fool."

"Thank you, Camilla."

I would love to hear what she was up to before raising Kingsley. She seems like a badass woman. I bet there's a hell of a lot of stories there.

She pats Kingsley on the shoulder and heads out the front door, giving me a secret wink on the way out that Kingsley doesn't notice. The door shuts behind her, leaving Kingsley and me alone.

"She likes you," Kingsley tells me when she's gone. "I've never seen her smile so much before in my life. And she actually invited you to the manor house. That's super rare."

"What can I say?" I reply. "I'm a pretty loveable person, aren't I?"

Before I can sit back down, he turns and puts his hands on my shoulders.

"Scarlett, I need to ask a favor from you."

34

KINGSLEY

"Okay, it's a bit of a strange request," I say.

Scarlett looks up at me, curious. "What is it?"

I sigh and lean in closer.

"I need you to help me with an audition."

Scarlett blinks. "An audition?"

"Yeah. A big Hollywood one."

"Kingsley, I can't fly to LA," Scarlett replies, distress written across her face.

She actually thinks I'm about to bundle her onto a plane.

I laugh. "No, that's not what I mean. I need you to *film* my audition. A self-tape. No flying."

Scarlett pouts, thinking. She looks so damn adorable this morning. All warm and soft. I have a strong urge to throw her over my shoulder and take her straight to bed right now to cuddle her tiny body all day, which is super weird because I've never felt like doing that with a girl. I'm the type to just send them on their way as soon as the sun rises.

I mean, I've been good to go since I rocked up to her flat's front door last night and saw her wearing that fucking irresistible dress. I would've ripped off that dress when we kissed on my sofa if she'd let me.

But Scarlett is different from other girls I've had before. I actually want to spend my time with her, and not just the kind that gets my dick wet. I want to get to know her fully. Wow.

You've gone soft, King. She's really got to your head, hasn't she?

I would have normally fucked my date by this point, but not Scarlett. I have never waited this long for a fucking girl.

But Scarlett is worth it.

"Okay," she replies. "Film your audition? Easy enough."

"And I need you to read the other character's lines."

Her face drops at my request, just as I fear.

"Oh."

"I seem to remember you being a good actress back in Crystal River," I reply. "How about you give this a go?"

"Hm. I remember you trying to put your tongue down my mouth more than performing."

"I'm a method actor, Scarlett. Always have been. Shakespeare explicitly told me to kiss Juliet, so that meant I just had to kiss you."

"That sounds like very *difficult* stage directions. It must've been so *hard* for you."

"Are you going to help me with this self-tape or what?" I ask. I really want her to say yes, just so that means she stays here in my apartment. I don't want her to leave. Not yet.

Am I really turning soft now for a girl? For Scarlett? Have I lost my mind?

If only Duke could see what's happening...

Scarlett pulls away from my hands on her shoulders and taps her lips absentmindedly, thinking. I see the request turning in her mind. She looks so damn sexy. Call me a fucking sapiosexual because I love the way this girl thinks.

"Hollywood, you say?"

"It's really big. It'll be one of the biggest films next year. Getting the lead in this film would launch me into the stratosphere."

"Good director?"

"He's a big up-and-comer. Very passionate. The part's perfect for me."

"Perfect in what way?"

"Oh, you know," I say casually. "Tall. Incredibly good-looking. Stylish. British."

She scoffs. "So, yeah, *nothing* like you at all."

"Put away that sharp tongue of yours, Scarlett."

"Make me."

"Oh, I will."

"You'll have to pay me," she says. "For me to even *consider* doing this thing."

"You can't be serious."

"This is my time. My services. You gotta pay me. I'm not doing this for nothing."

She gives me a steely look.

She's so damn hot negotiating like this. So serious and firm with me.

I feel my cock twitch in agreement.

She's not making things easy for me, isn't she? Any other girl I would've fucked last night, but Scarlett wants more from me than just my money thrown at her and a flashy car. I know she wants me to prove myself to her.

"This will only take an hour or less. How much are you thinking of?"

I check the time. My Hollywood agent said that the director will call me in twenty minutes for the audition. I need to get this sorted.

Scarlett sways on her feet and cheekily smiles. "I'd say a thousand pounds should cover it, considering how much of a big deal you're making it out to be."

One thousand pounds?

Fuck it.

I'm loaded. I can easily afford this without a second's thought.

"Deal," I say.

Her eyes widen. "What? Really?"

"Sure. If that's how much you value your services."

"I just came up with a big number, that's all."

I shrug. "I'm willing to pay it. I need someone to read the lines."

"Someone, or *me* specifically?"

Of course I want you, Scarlett. Can't you see that?

"You're the only one I can see in this apartment."

"Gosh, well... now I feel pressure to live up to a thousand British pounds of acting ability."

"I'm sure you'll be great," I say teasingly. "Although, if I don't get this job, then I will definitely put the entirety of the blame on you."

Scarlett gulps and I smile.

* * *

"So, Ryan, my friend here is going to read the other character's lines, if that's alright?"

The director gives me an enthusiastic thumbs up through the computer screen.

"Sounds great."

"She's American, like you."

"Even better."

I look up at Scarlett. My temporary co-star. She's deliberately behind my computer so that she can't be seen, cringing hard. I throw her a smirk and she rolls her eyes in response.

"I'm ready to just launch into it if you are," I say to Ryan, preparing myself to give a good performance.

"Go ahead."

We run through the scene with the director nodding along on the screen and Scarlett reading in as the other girl. The girl I have to seduce. I look her directly in the eyes as I speak my lines. They're so well written. The scene is about a lothario sweet-talking an innocent virgin. It's all incredibly sexy. Scarlett's cheeks flush with color every time she looks up from her script. I see her tremble at my dirty words. It goes beyond the point of whether it's even the script talking anymore or myself to Scarlett.

It makes the performance very *realistic*, to say the least.

"How about I take you out back and we play around? You'll like that, won't you? I know what you want."

Ha. These lines.

Doing this takes me back to Crystal River. Back to the best night of my life when it was just Scarlett and Shakespeare and me with the world at our feet. I remember wanting that night to last forever.

"You and I are going to get *very* close. It's inevitable. You and I are bound together forever. I've been lusting after you and your body for quite some time, girl. Give yourself over to me."

Despite my naughty glances down at her incredible body during the scene, I am in total awe of Scarlett. Here is the woman whose heart I broke, who came to London to pursue her dreams with no money in her pocket, and she has put aside her self-consciousness to try her best to help me with this audition. And all I'm doing is shooting her seductive glances that obviously make her sweet pussy wet.

If that's what I can do with just my face and my voice, just imagine what I can do with my cock.

I think that same thought passes through her mind. She can't hold eye contact with me at all. I see her lick her lips, and it's not because they're dry.

"I'm going to lick you up and down until you scream my name, begging me to stop."

We have to do the scene three times. I really enjoy it. Scarlett can't seem to bear it.

"Great," Ryan says. "We've got everything we need there. We'll be in contact with your agent."

"Thanks."

"Your American friend was excellent, by the way. So believable as a woman being seduced. Is she an actress? She should definitely consider it."

Scarlett squeaks in gratefulness before the director hangs up. It's very cute.

"So, what happens now, *Mr. Movie Star*?" Scarlett asks me as I turn off the computer.

"We just have to wait," I reply, loving the way her new nickname for me falls off her tongue.

"Oh."

I stroke her arm. "Thank you for that. I'll send you the money as soon as possible."

Scarlett blushes, which somehow makes her even more adorable.

"You know, I was only joking about the money," she says.

I gently pull her in close to me. She lets me. I feel her warm body go soft at my control. She looks so hot in my old hoodie. With my name written across the hoodie, it makes her seem like she's mine.

I wish she is.

"Kingsley," she whispers as our legs touch under the table. I wish she calls me *King*. That would really send me over the edge.

"I want you," I say. I can't deny it anymore. I just have to have her. Make her truly mine. She softly gasps at my words, and I feel her body shudder. I bring her head towards me.

"This is too fast," she says. "You just sprung back into my life so quickly, I don't know what to think."

"You don't want this?" I ask. It comes out as a deep growl.

Scarlett garbles her words. She's hesitant, so I let her go.

There's plenty of time to convince her that we belong together, but now is not that moment. It pains me to know that.

But I can wait. I can pursue at my own pace.

She's the only thing I think about. My American girl I let go once and who I'm never going to let go again. She will be mine. Soon. When she comes to me.

"I need time," she says, almost trying to come up with an excuse. But I understand. I would be confused too if I were in her position. I wouldn't trust myself.

"Just know that I want you, Scarlett. You and only you. You got that?"

She can't resist. She leans forward and gives me a quick kiss on the lips. It's like a taster of her. Something that makes my body stiffen.

She will come to her senses soon enough. She'll know I want just her.

"I gotta go," she says. "My flatmate will be wondering where I am. She's probably called the cops on you already."

"It's okay. Go."

I watch her gather her things and dash out the door,

giving me one last fleeting glance before she leaves. A look that tells me she's already mine; she just doesn't know it yet.

It's true what I told her. I want her. And, like it was at Crystal River High, I'm not going to stop until she's mine.

35

SCARLETT

GRACE LEADS us down a dark alley. It feels very unsafe down here, even by London standards. Ominous. Very Victorian.

I have a bad sense as we navigate down this tight space. It's like something bad haunts this place. My skin crawls, and it isn't long until I find out why.

"This is where it happened," Grace says with a very serious and very uncharacteristic tone. "The *murder*."

The crowd around me gasps. A bunch of violence-hungry onlookers.

We're on Grace's Jack the Ripper Tour.

The group eagerly laps up all the gory details and my flatmate's brilliant retelling of them. They have done so with every one of the Ripper's murder sites we've walked to this evening in Whitechapel.

At Grace's insistent invitation, I've tagged along as a spectator.

And, I must say, I'm really *bloody* enjoying it, to use one of Grace's phrases.

"Imagine what Whitechapel would've been like a few hundred years ago," Grace continues to tell her enraptured audience in the cramped dark alley. "This area, right in the East End of London, was the slums of the city. Prostitutes. Thugs. Gangs. Back then, even police were afraid to go down these very streets we're walking on tonight. No wonder one man was able to get away with murdering so many women."

Grace's storytelling makes me squirm, which I guess is exactly what she wants.

She really is amazing.

We continue down the narrow streets of the East End with Grace pointing out all the different murder sites. I can imagine being here all those years ago. Penniless. In the dim light of candles. Policemen with whistles in the fog. A murderer on the loose.

No wonder Grace loves doing these tours.

When the tour ends by the Tube Station, I wait behind for Grace to finish receiving thanks from all the members of her audience. I watch her receive a whole load of tips. She's pocketing so much dough, and no surprise with the performance she just gave these tourists.

"Pub?" she asks me when she's finally done talking to her customers.

I nod. "Pub."

We head into the nearest place. A proper old-school boozer. I can imagine this place existing back when Jack himself stalked these streets, full of drunken sailors and ladies of the night.

I buy her a glass of wine and we sit down by the window. Night falls on London outside.

"What did you think?" Grace asks in a rare moment of

vulnerability from her. She taps her glass, nervous for my answer.

"You really are the best tour guide in the whole city," I say, and it's true.

Her face launches into a big smile.

"Oh, I'm glad you liked it! I thought it might be too... *violent* for you."

"No, I love seeing this side of London. And you do such a good job, Grace. I had a great time. You've really introduced me to the cool parts of London."

"Thanks."

We chink our glasses together and drink.

But watching Grace work wasn't the only reason I came tonight. I need her help to talk over things with her. She's the only person I know in this city, and the only person I know best suited to give me honest no-nonsense advice.

"You remember that guy from the press party the other night?" I ask her, finally summoning up the courage to speak to her about this.

She nods. "The one who asked you out on that date?"

"Yeah, him. Well, I did go out on that date with him."

She leans forward, excited and curious. "Oh, please. Tell me *everything*."

I had told her I was going out with Kingsley the night he took me to the British Library. I didn't give her too many details about it, though. I never told her that he was the guy I told her about in the bar in Soho. She doesn't know he's the boy from my past who broke my heart.

"Well, I actually know him from before."

"Before? From when?"

"From before I even came to London. Crystal River High. He was *that* boy. The posh one who came to America and who... screwed me about."

Grace smiles. She's loving this. "No bloody way," she exclaims.

She's beside herself.

"Oh, yes."

"Didn't I tell you that you might run into him, being in this city? And now you actually freaking *have*. Oh, Scarlett, this is fantastic. Simply bloody fantastic. You're making me feel all giddy."

"That's not making things better, Grace."

"Please keep talking, this is *so* juicy. Tell me again how you two first met. I am so invested now. Don't skip a single thing."

And I do. I tell her about Kingsley and me in my bedroom back in Crystal River. I do leave out the... *sexual* details of what went down between us, though. Grace laps it all up like she's watching a riveting reality TV show. She bites her lip as I tell her about how he disappeared overnight and then turned up four years later at the theater I work at.

"This is crazy," Grace says when I come to the end of my story. "I was only joking when I said you might run into him here. I never thought it would actually bloody happen!"

"And then we went on a date the other night and I ended up at his place."

"No way. What happened? Did you guys... *do it*?"

"We kissed, that's all."

"Nothing... *deeper*? Please tell me you went all the way."

"Grace, nothing else occurred between us."

She seems downhearted. "Oh, what a shame."

"And now I don't know what to do."

Grace thinks for a moment. Taking it all in. She shakes her head at me.

"You're such a naughty minx, Scarlett."

I roll my eyes. "Tell me about it."

"I honestly don't know what you should do."

"Come on, Grace," I plead. "You're the best person for this. You never give a shit. You're the coolest person I know. What would you do?"

"You know I'm not always like this," she replies. "I've had my own heartbreak, but if I was going to say anything, it's that this guy seems to be apologetic over what happened between you two. He's clearly trying to make amends for his asshole behavior. Oh, and he's rich. That is definitely a bonus. But whatever you decide to do, make sure it's your own decision, Scarlett. That it's what *you* want to do."

"Gotcha."

"Don't let anyone tell you what you should do. It's your life, girl. If you think this guy is worth your time, then go for him with everything you have."

"And what happened with you?" I ask. "Your heartbreak? How did you deal with it?"

"I never got over it," she says, sighing. "That's the thing with loving someone hard. You never get over it. You learn to live with it, and if you get a second chance with them, then you have to decide what you truly want. Me? I've made the decision a long time ago that it will take a real man to control my heart. I won't let anyone through. I like my independence, and the man who pursues me will have to learn to live with it before I even consider him."

"See? You're so cool," I exclaim. "I wish I had half the backbone you have, Grace."

"Scarlett, you definitely do. You don't know how strong you really are."

"Maybe," I blush, taking a long sip of wine.

"You're definitely taking this guy for a spin, that's for sure," she says.

"I just want to make sure he's the real deal."

"I don't blame you, but tell me, Scarlett," Grace says in an even more serious tone than she did during her tour. "With this man, what do you really want?"

I pause for a very long time. Thinking of Kingsley. How he makes me feel. How my body reacts whenever he walks into a room I'm in and looks at me with his striking eyes. How his touch makes me melt.

"I want him," I say finally. It's weird to say those words out loud, but I know they're true the minute they leave my mouth.

"Then go get him," Grace says. "Make him yours."

36

SCARLETT

GRACE IS RIGHT.

I gotta make Kingsley mine. It's what I really desire.

I've got to be strong and get what I want. I can't put this off any longer. It's time to face the truth.

With this realization, I leave the pub with a new inner purpose and drive.

Which is probably why I head straight to his dressing room the next day after the show, bursting with newfound confidence. All night long, I've been dreaming of Kingsley and me. Us two together.

I think of what I'm going to say to him. How I'm going to tell him that he has my heart, no matter how much I've tried to keep it sealed off. He's had my heart for years.

And if he's ready, then I will be his. I believe we should be together.

He told me he wanted me the other night, but that's only if he can promise he won't mess me around. I'm a self-respecting girl enough to ask for everything or nothing, and that's what I'm going to ask him now.

If he doesn't want me - if he can't commit - then fine. I'll walk away. I'll get a new job. I'll be in pain, but I will learn to live without him. I'll just get it done now rather than hold on to false hope for another four years.

Things have to come to a head, and I'm prepared to be the one who'll force it.

I'm nervous but excited. This could be the start of a new life.

This might be the beginning of my future.

At the theater, I head backstage after the show's end. I find his dressing room.

I take in a deep breath as I stand outside his door, ready to knock. Surely, he's still in there; the performance has only just wrapped up.

But I hear voices coming from inside. Someone else is in there with him, and all the confidence I've just pumped myself up with immediately floods out of my body.

I recognize that voice; I hear it every night from the stage.

It's Penelope Jellis.

She's talking. Loudly.

I press my ear up against the dressing room door to hear properly. I'm curious as to what she's talking to Kingsley about.

She's talking about *me*.

"Honestly, King, I don't know what you see in her. You're rich, and she's just some American chick who probably lives in some shared house."

"No," I whisper to myself.

She's really laying into me...

"What are you doing with her? You know where this can only lead," Penelope continues. "You're going to play around with her and then you're going to break her heart. You know that's the case, just accept it. You're being cruel to the poor girl."

I hear Kingsley's voice. He's quieter than the actress. More restrained.

"No, Penelope..."

"Look at your family name, King. You're a *Heath-Harding*, for goodness' sake. A proper noble. Posh. You're in line to inherit a historic estate. In a truthful world, you would have nothing to do with some small town American girl, just admit it. You two are worlds apart."

I pull my ear away from the door. I've heard enough.

And I agree with Penelope.

It's a harsh truth, but that doesn't make it any less real.

Tears sting my eyes.

No matter how snobby or downright awful she is, Penelope does have a point. Both Kingsley and I are deluding ourselves with what we have. It's clear he'll have to take up his responsibility as a Heath-Harding and leave me, just like he did four years ago. After all, I am just a poor American girl. Who am I to him, really? A fling? A fun time? I'm not nobility. Hell, I'm not even *English*. Kingsley might be saying all the right words now, but sooner or later, he'll go back to his world. He *has* to. It's in his blue blood.

And I can't blame him.

Neither he nor I can fight hundreds of years of history or ancient British tradition handed down generations. Even love can't fight something so entrenched.

Really, he should be with another aristocrat with super-model looks. Someone like Penelope Jellis.

These are the doubts I've been mulling over in my head for days. It just takes Penelope to say them out loud for them to become real. The London Grand Hotel. The Palace nightclub. The private tour of the British Library.

The amazing penthouse apartment over Tower Bridge. I should not be in this world. I've just been a tourist flying through, and I can never stay.

Kingsley and I are not meant to be together. I was living a fantasy dreaming that we could.

I suddenly no longer have the confidence with which I strolled backstage with. I've completely lost my zeal now as I stand here on the other side of his door. With Penelope's words, I feel like I'm sealed off from him forever.

I better face up to the truth that Kingsley and I can't be together.

I better just leave and forget about him. Stop all this before it hurts too much.

Well, it's too late. It's going to hurt. It's already hurting.

But at least I'm the one now that gets to turn around and go on my own terms this time. I'm the one to decide my own destiny.

And that's exactly what I do.

With tears streaming, I walk away from Kingsley's dressing room. I'm going to leave this theater and never come back.

I'm going to never see Kingsley again. It's the only way.

I KNEW I was going to make Scarlett and Kingsley feel real pain, and now I had come up with a plan on exactly how to.

I was in the theater they both work in, and the best thing was that they both didn't know I was in there. They had no fucking clue about what I was doing. The simple idea of that thrilled me all over as I waited for them.

They were both in the building, that I knew. Oh, how fun it was going to be to commit my crime so close to them.

That'll teach them. That'll make them feel real pain.

The night's performance was long over by the time I decide to enact my plan. They were still in the theater. Scarlett was going backstage to his dressing room. There weren't many other people around. Everything was perfect.

It made me giggle. I couldn't control myself.

I usually don't take pride in what I do, but that night I allowed myself some enjoyment.

Now I knew it was my time to strike.

37

KINGSLEY

Well, Penelope pisses me off. Big fucking time.

To even barge into my backstage dressing room like this pisses me off enough, let alone all her unsolicited talk about Scarlett that she just unloads on me.

"You have no right to talk about this," I interrupt her little spiel. I keep my voice low. I'm not raising my energy to meet hers.

How dare she talk about my girl like that? How dare she assume I'm on the same page as her when it comes to my family?

Penelope came into my dressing room like a ball of raging fire. She's all big arm gestures and facial expressions. Watching her get all worked up reminds me of a shop mannequin placed in a ridiculous pose. Plastic and fake.

I see her game plan. She wants to pull Scarlett and me apart. She talks about my family background. About how Scarlett and I are worlds apart.

She has no fucking clue what I think. She doesn't know me. Not in the way Scarlett does.

It makes me angry. Real fucking angry.

"Stop talking," I command her eventually, cutting her short. I've heard enough.

"But *King*..."

I growl. "Enough. You're overstepping yourself here, Penelope."

She ignores me. Man, she is insistent.

What's she doing now?

Penelope swans across my dressing room towards me like a dart. She changes her tone and posture in an instant, like the talented actress she is. She becomes soft. Doe-like eyes. Her hands find mine.

"Oh, King."

Her voice is very sultry. I can see this trick working on a lot of men.

Not me, though.

"What?"

"You know, I just did a big interview with *The Times* yesterday."

"I didn't read it."

"Can you guess what most of the questions were about?"

"No," I reply. Her hands tighten around mine. She leans closer. I can smell her lavender perfume. Strong and very expensive.

"They were about *us*, King. About how much we click on stage. About all the rumors flying around town about us. You know, half of London thinks we're together."

"Right."

"So," Penelope says, walking her fingers seductively up along my thick biceps to my shoulder. "How about you ask me out on a date? How about I say *yes*?"

Right then, there's a loud and urgent knock on my dressing room door, saving my ass. It gives me enough reason to push Penelope away from my body.

A bit of me actually hopes that Scarlett is at the door. I would really like to see her. I want to talk to her about the other night. She's the only girl I want to take out on a date.

But it's not her.

It's Steve, our play's director. He's standing there with two austere-looking policemen behind him. It is an unusual sight to see policemen in a theater, to say the least.

What are they doing here?

It must be something serious.

"What is it?" I ask. "What's happened?"

38

SCARLETT

YEP. *That's it. I've made up my mind.*

I can't ever see Kingsley again.

I'll send him a letter, though. I won't run away as he did. I'll explain my reasoning. I'll explain our differences. I'll explain how illogical our pairing will be, despite what my heart tells me.

It's the only way all this can be resolved.

In order to get over him, I'm going to have to break my own heart.

I walk down Shaftesbury Avenue away from the Prestige Theater, tears stinging my eyes.

I see flashing blue lights. Police cars heading in the opposite direction. Police cars that stop outside the theater I've just come from.

There's a lot of them.

Something is happening.

Something is wrong.

I turn to go back. A swarm of policemen gathers outside

the building I just stepped out of, and all I can think is one thing.

Kingsley is in there.

Has something happened to him? Why are the police here? Why are their sirens on?

I break into a run back to where I just came.

The police are already cordoning off the theater by the time I reach the building, putting up blue tape and stopping traffic down Shaftesbury Avenue.

In the panic, I see Giles stumbling out of a side door of the theater, ashen-faced.

"What is wrong?" I ask him, out of breath from my sprint. "Are you okay, Giles?"

He turns to me. He has a thousand-mile stare. Like he's seen a ghost.

"Scarlett," he says. "There's been a murder."

39

SCARLETT

I shut the door to my flat and just stand there in shock. I don't make an attempt to move into the living room. I just drop my bag to the floor and shake my head in disbelief at how my evening has panned out.

"You would not believe what happened to me today," Grace calls out from the kitchen, completely oblivious to my emotional state. "I went to the park, right? Bought a sandwich and I sat down on a bench. All fine. And then a pigeon shat on me. All over. I was covered in it, but you know what? I said, fine. Went to get napkins and rubbed the shit off me. But then I sat back down on the same bench and, I'm not kidding you, *five minutes later* another pigeon flew by and shat on me. *Again.* Twice in ten minutes, you can't make this stuff up. I guess it means good luck, right? So, if I was double-shat on then that should mean I get double the luck, yeah? I could really do with some."

She barges into the hallway, wiping down a tea mug with tea towel, expecting an answer from me.

But then she sees me. She sees the color drained from my face. She immediately stops everything.

"What happened?" Grace asks me. "What are you looking so shocked by?"

"Someone's been murdered at my work," I reply quietly. I shake my head again.

Grace frowns. "What?"

"A murder. At my work."

She goes straight into action mode.

"Sit down, Scarlett. Tell me everything about it."

With her hands on my shoulder, she gently ushers me into the living room and onto the sofa.

"It happened tonight," I mutter. "I can't believe it. I must've been in the building when it happened."

"Okay. I'm going to make you some tea," she says.

Of course. The British way of dealing with any crises. *A nice cup of tea.*

But I don't complain. I need a cup of tea right now. Maybe even something a little stronger.

Grace puts on the kettle and rejoins me on the sofa. I'm glad she's next to me. I'm glad I can talk to her about this.

"Are you okay?" she asks.

I nod slowly. "I'm okay. I think."

"Do you want to talk about it?"

I wipe away tears from my cheeks. "Yes."

"Okay. I'm here. I'm listening."

"Do you remember that guy from the press party at the Tower of London?" I ask her. "That silent guy who spoke to Kingsley? I think his name was Ben Helper?"

Grace squints her eyes. "Maybe."

"Well, he was murdered tonight. On the actual stage of the theater. It must've happened just as I was leaving. Someone's killed him. The police are treating it as a full-blown thing."

Grace leans back.

"Bloody hell."

"His body was found on the stage, just covered in blood."

"On the stage?"

"They say his throat had been slit. It sounds so violent."

"And you were in there? It could've been you."

I take in a deep breath.

"Oh, Grace. I don't even want to think that," I whisper, my voice trembling.

"I'm sorry, I didn't mean..."

"It's okay. I know. It's awful to think I was *there* when it was happening."

"Are you sure you're okay?" Grace asks, taking hold of my hands gently. "Do you need anything? Can I help you in any way?"

"I'm just a bit shaken," I say. "I just need some time to compose myself."

"This is crazy," my flatmate says. In the kitchen, the kettle finishes boiling, but she makes no move for it. "What are you going to do?"

For the third time tonight, I just shake my head.

"I don't know."

40

SCARLETT

IT'S BEEN one week since that terrible night and I have not seen Kingsley since. Every day I have turned on the news to see more stories about the murder. About the investigation. About Kingsley.

It was his publicist that had been so violently murdered, so all the press coverage has centered ruthlessly on the young star. Digging through Kingsley's past life. His exes. The whole thing.

Thank God no sniffing journalist has been able to unearth anything about me.

I've barely been able to sleep or to eat in the last week. I didn't even know Ben, but I have been worried sick for Kingsley and for what he's going through. Not only he's had to deal with grieving a friend, but he's also had to face the relentless British tabloids.

Oh, the story is juicy for prying journalists, that's for sure.

And I've missed the man. So freaking much. It's only been one week, but it's like we've been apart for another four years. I can't comfort him in his time of need.

Which has led to me - exactly one week since I rushed back to the theater to hear about the murder - to ring the buzzer to Kingsley's penthouse.

I had made a decision to leave him, but that was before all this. I know I can't disappear now, not when he's probably in pain and vulnerable. I would never be able to live with myself. All week, I've felt this intense protective urge over Kingsley. No matter what he did four years ago, the last few weeks he's been so good to me.

I know that he needs me now, more than ever.

"I'm not seeing anyone."

Kingsley's voice comes through the buzzer, loud and clear. He's stern. Angry.

I can't blame him. I bet he's been harassed all week.

"It's me," I say into the intercom.

"Hello?"

"It's Scarlett. I know you're not seeing anyone, but what about me?"

"Come on up."

Thank God.

The door automatically swings open, and I head inside. I ride up the elevator all the way to his top floor.

Kingsley is waiting for me in the private lobby of his penthouse.

He looks disheveled. Messy hair. Bags under the eyes. Somehow, Kingsley makes a sleepless and stressful week look super sexy.

"Hey," he says when the elevator doors open.

I tentatively approach. "Hi. You okay? I didn't know whether to come."

And then, unexpectedly, Kingsley wraps his arms around me and brings me in for a tight hug.

"I've been waiting for you," he whispers into my hair. "I've wanted to see you all week."

My heart melts.

"I brought flowers," I say, waving the bouquet I just bought.

Kingsley smiles. "Thanks. Add them to the collection."

He gestures into the spare room. It's full of flowers. The man must know half of London.

"Oh."

"It's... a lot," Kingsley says, rolling his eyes. "No one ever warns you that one of the hardest things dealing with a murder of a friend is the sheer amount of flowers everyone sends you."

"You look exhausted," I say, taking his hand. His grip is soft. "I'll make you a cup of tea."

I resort to the British method of dealing with a crisis. Grace has taught me well.

Kingsley sits down in his living room while I make him a cup of tea. It's the first time I've ever made one. It's a minor disaster.

The look on Kingsley's face when he sips it reaffirms my judgment. He scrunches up his cheeks.

"It's good," he lies, before bravely taking another sip.

I can't watch the poor man torture himself for my dignity anymore.

"I can tell it's bad. It's okay, you don't have to drink anymore."

Kingsley immediately puts the cup on the table as if it's a ticking time bomb.

"Thank God. I feel like you were trying to poison me there, darling."

I laugh. "I'm glad you're smiling."

"It's been the first time I've smiled in a week," Kingsley tells me. "Thank you for surprising me today. I don't know how many more days I could've coped without seeing your gorgeous face."

"Maybe you need something more powerful than an American-made tea," I suggest. "Do you have any more of that Scotch from the other night?"

"That is a very good idea." He nods towards the kitchen. "Top cupboard."

I fetch us two glasses of the strong stuff. One shot of it certainly wakes me up.

"How has last week been?" I ask him as the alcohol hits my system like hot lava. "What happened at the theater? How's the investigation going? It just sounds so insane. Who would want to do something like that? Sorry, I must be asking so many insensitive questions."

Kingsley shakes his head. "No, don't apologize. I like it that you're here."

"I just hear so much horrible stuff through the news."

"Yeah, the paparazzi have not been very kind," Kingsley says.

"That's an understatement."

"No one knows who murdered Ben, not even the police," he explains. "Not one single clue. It's like a ghost has floated in and done it."

"Do you think it was some crazy person?"

"Whoever did this was methodical. The whole act was pre-meditated. No one can slip into a theater like that and murder someone on the stage so dramatically without a plan. They have simply left no evidence at all."

"That's insane," I say. "How are you holding up?"

Kingsley sighs and downs the rest of his Scotch. "It seems like everyone wants a piece of me just because I'm in connection with Ben. It's like everyone's forgotten completely about him and is obsessed with my reaction to his murder. It's like he's never existed and it's all about me. I hate it. I just want everyone to know that Ben was a real person with a story. You can't erase all that in favor of his celebrity employer."

I reach for his hand. "It must've been so hard for you."

Kingsley turns to me. "Thank you again for coming, Scarlett."

"Of course I came."

"You know that you're the first girl who just likes me for who I am and not for some celebrity status? You knew me long before I was famous. You didn't know or care about my family name when we met, unlike so many of my so-called *friends*. Best of all, you're the only person I know who wouldn't be super apologetic that you've made me a terrible cup of tea."

I roll my eyes. "It wasn't *that* bad."

"Scarlett, I'm sure that cup of tea wouldn't even fit under the definition of drinkable in the dictionary."

I laugh again, and we spend the next few hours talking and drinking the rest of the bottle of Scotch. It's past midnight that we both start to yawn.

"I think I should go," I announce, rubbing my tired eyes. "It's getting late. I can't stay over again and push into your hospitality."

Kingsley ignores me.

"I think I must've been the target," he says under his breath.

"Pardon?"

"The target for whoever murdered Ben. I feel like he must've been after me. There's no reason why anyone would target Ben."

"How do you know?" I ask him. "You can't possibly have guessed that."

"I just know," Kingsley replies softly. "He was after me. I was the target. That murder was just a message. He's coming for me."

And, deep down, I know he is right.

And it feels me with terror.

41

SCARLETT

THE EARLY MORNING sun is just creeping through Kingsley's bedroom window when he enters.

Like the last time I was over, I've spent the night sleeping in his bed whilst he's slept on the living room sofa. And, just like last time, the impulse to visit Kingsley in the middle of the night was nearly overpowering. I was so close to giving in all night.

But, when the bedroom door creaks open as sunlight hits my pillow in the morning, I know that it's Kingsley who has been the first of us to give in to desire.

I close my eyes and pretend to still be asleep, but Kingsley sees right through my little ruse.

I sense him cross the room and approach the bed slowly, reminding me of a wild predator single-mindedly stalking his prey in the long grass. This is a man who gets what he wants.

And, right now, he wants me.

As Kingsley's hot, strong hands touch the back of my

bare legs, making me involuntarily shiver, he leans forward and whispers my name. His breath blows against the skin on my neck.

"Scarlett."

Fuck, the man's liquid-smooth voice seeps deep into my body. I long for him.

I can barely keep my eyes shut as Kingsley's fingers delicately - *teasingly* - run up my legs towards my barely concealed ass. I bite my lip involuntarily.

I've slept naked, and as Kingsley's hands reach my exposed ass crack, I can practically *hear* the man's cock go hard in his quivering voice.

"Oh, *Scarlett*."

He wants to feel me. His fingers dance on my firm ass cheeks for a brief moment before I feel his erect cock press into my leg as he climbs on top of me.

God, this man can't be stopped.

I can't resist any longer. I eagerly turn my head to kiss the man, but my mouth immediately fills not with his lips but with Kingsley's thumb. He makes me suck on it, and I greedily do so with a vigorous moan. I *really* want to say his name, but my mouth is full.

My whole body is burning with an uncontrollable thirst for this man who has haunted my dreams for four long years. Right now, I will taste anything of his he puts into my mouth.

Kingsley's spare hand finds my opening between my legs. It isn't hard for him. My pussy is *soaking* wet and aching for his manly touch.

Oh, God. This is too much.

I suckle even harder on Kingsley's thumb as he lightly plays around my sex, tormenting me. All I want is for him to fill me up with his thick member, but I know I have no control here. He's going to mess with me until he's ready to fuck me properly. I have no choice and it sends me wild. He's playing me like a fiddle, knowing exactly what to do to bring me to the point of frustrating climax.

The man is aggressive and controlling. Dominating my body. I just give in to him and let him be the one to take charge. I remember how it was four years ago. How he owned me then.

He really can't be stopped.

"Scarlett," he whispers again. He's panting. My body is making him exhausted. I bet he's been thinking of doing exactly this to me for such a long time, just like I have.

He can do whatever he wants to me.

I moan again, practically begging him to fuck me.

"Such a naughty girl to reject me so many times," he says. "Thinking you are stronger than this. I knew you'll give in to me, eventually. You're all mine."

I pull my mouth from his thumb. "Who says I've given into you, Kingsley? You haven't even fucked me properly yet. Stop playing with me and take me like a man, and then I might give into you."

He growls like an angry animal at my reply and then flips my body around so that I'm facing him. He spins me like I weigh nothing. His muscles glisten with sweat in the sunlight as his eyes burn with lust for me.

He's vicious.

He still doesn't fuck me, though. Not in the way that I want. Instead, he goes for my throbbing clit.

I can't take this teasing anymore.

My legs lock together, and warmth fills my belly.

"I want you inside me," I groan. "Fuck me like a man."

Kingsley bares his white teeth at me. "Beg for it, Scarlett."

"Please, Kingsley."

"Oh, I'm going to fuck you. I want to see you shake from just my little finger."

Fuck. This man makes me bite hard into his bedsheets to stop myself from screaming out his name in pleasure.

And then, as I reach a point where my whole body feels like it's on fire, he enters me. And I fill with *him.* I let out a satisfied whimper as he goes deep inside me. I feel stuffed. His insatiable desire for me makes me shiver.

Kingsley roughly kisses my neck as he pins my wrists above my head with just one hand. His body grinds against me as he furiously fucks me. My back arches as he pounds me. I try to break my hands free, just to see how strong he is, but my wrists don't even move under his iron grip.

He's right. I'm all his.

His grunting turns me on even more. I gasp. As he fucks me, he continues to play with my clit with his spare hand. I can't bear it anymore.

He brings me to orgasm.

"My naughty girl," he whispers. "This is how a real man fucks."

Yep, this is definitely the way I want to be fucked.

My leg shakes as my world explodes, just as he said it would. I see the gleam of delight in his eyes as he watches me finally succumb to my desire. *He's* made me feel like this with just his touch and the feel of his massive cock inside me. It's beyond anything I ever imagined. It's like I'm giving my whole soul over to this man.

"Oh, Kingsley."

He grunts and plows deep inside me. He bites at my ear until he finishes, yelling my name out with a low moan.

"*Scarlett...*"

He rests down on top of me, spent. I'm frozen in place, unable to move because of simply how *good* I feel. An inner glow builds up inside my chest. My fingers trace down his back and I feel his sweat.

"You look so sexy when you're sweaty," I say to the man as he breathes deeply next to my neck.

He lifts his head up to face me and gives me a kiss. His hair is so wet. Gorgeous. I want to soak in his sweat.

"You look so sexy when you're *naked*," he replies. "How could I resist you when you sleep completely bare like that?"

I wrap my arms around him. "I don't want you to resist me anymore."

"Good," he says with a devious smile. "Because I'm ready for round two."

42

SCARLETT

Kingsley snoozes next to me as I rub his toned back, feeling his firm muscles. The man must work out as an absolute beast every single day to have such a hot body. But, despite his overwhelming strength, he looks so peaceful asleep. I run my finger along his perfect jawline and touch his full lips. I bite my own, still so freaking horny for him even though I've had him pound me just minutes ago.

I rest my head on the soft pillow and just bathe in that satisfying post-sex glow. A pleasurable tingle flows up from between my legs as I think of Kingsley leaning over me, sweat dripping from his wet curly hair, as he screwed my body into oblivion. I'm so warm and tired in that lovely way that only happens when you've been fucked hard.

I exhale and lean over to the side of the bed to check my phone. The news is full of articles about the theater murder.

Oh. Right.

In the passion of last night and this morning, I've completely forgotten about all that.

Next to me, Kingsley stirs. He opens one eye to see me scrolling through my phone.

"Fuck, they're still talking about last week?" he asks.

"Yep. They really are like vultures."

"I've not expected anything less from them. The British press has hounded my family for years."

"I'm sorry to see you go through this," I say.

"Thanks for coming over, Scarlett. You've made me feel a damn lot better."

He lifts his face to kiss me gently on the forehead, and it's like stars burst in my stomach.

I can't handle him.

"They're never going to stop," I say, nodding at the phone.

"Nope. Not until they've rung this thing out for every last penny. I hate journalists. Someone has literally just died and all they want to do is provoke and prod."

I glance at the time.

"I better go," I say. "I bet you have a busy day dealing with all this crap."

Kingsley sighs. "Yeah, I've gotta talk to the police today. Again."

"I bet that's annoying."

"I'd prefer you to stay, though. I need you."

He needs me?

Those are words I've wished to hear, because - *damn* - I need him.

He might've just fucked me in his own bed, but I've still got enough spark and independence to tease him.

"I've got things to do," I lie, sliding out of bed. I start to put my clothes on from yesterday.

I want to leave him wanting more.

Kingsley watches me dress, biting his lip. He really can't resist me, can't he?

Everything in my body screams at me to climb back into bed with him and demand him to fuck me again, but instead, I say my goodbyes.

"See you soon, Kingsley."

"I'll call you," he says. "You better pick up."

I wink before I head out of his penthouse.

On the elevator trip down, I adjust my skirt. I feel so dirty from last night. I haven't showered. I still feel him deep inside me. I've half-covered in his hot sweat.

It all turns me on.

I didn't plan on having sex when I arrived last night. Maybe I was just stupid and didn't truly realize how deep my feeling for Kingsley ran.

Maybe this might even be one of the last times I see him. I still can't forget the conversation I overheard backstage before the murder last week. What Penelope said about our irreconcilable differences. Kingsley might still retreat back into his own world.

But, for one fleeting moment, he was part of mine this morning.

Imagine what it'll be like with a man like Kingsley Heath-Harding. The kind of life I might lead.

I know I shouldn't dream about that, but my head wanders and my heart soars.

I don't have much time to dream. The elevator doors ping open, and I am greeted by a sudden flash of cameras.

I'm momentarily blinded by the surprising bright lights that it takes me a second to realize what's happening.

A whole swarm of paparazzi is stationed outside Kingsley's building, waiting to ambush whoever enters or leaves his apartment. And, right now, that's *me*.

There are more flashes. I raise my arm to block my face.

And then I hear one of the photographers call out to the others.

"Oh, don't worry. She's just the cleaner."

The photos stop.

The cleaner?

Is that what I look like to these men?

Well, compared to Kingsley Heath-Harding, *fair enough*. I guess it is his world and we're just living in it.

At least they don't suspect a thing. They don't even know that Kingsley was balls-deep in me just minutes ago. They think I'm a minimum-wage employee. I don't mind that.

It's just our little secret, and that is a major turn-on.

I roll my eyes at the paparazzi, but say nothing. I squeeze past them to head down the street. *What a close shave.*

The last thing I want is a photo of messy me leaving Kingsley's apartment splashed across the British tabloids. No way.

43

SCARLETT

I DON'T HEAR from Kingsley for three days.

Every scenario plays through my head in that time of radio silence. Maybe he's cut me out completely; it is to be expected. He's a guy, after all. He's been able to fuck me. He's moved on. That's what boys do.

And, plus, he's probably super busy with the murder case. And he's probably over me already.

And you know what? I'm okay with it. In the last few days, I've accepted whatever happens. It's painful, but I've been here before, so I know I can pick myself up from the ground. My life isn't ruined just because a guy doesn't want to talk to me.

I've also been busy trying to find another job, so I've been keeping myself busy with that. No matter what happens, I can't stay working at the Prestige Theater. It has temporarily shut down whilst the murder investigation has taken place, and I don't know how long that'll go on for. So, I need to find another job.

Grace has offered to help me put a good word in to be a tour guide for the company she works for, but I politely declined. I know I'll feel like some imposter as an American girl telling American tourists about a British city. Besides, I'm not nearly as extroverted as Grace is. I can't do public speaking.

Or maybe I'm just lying to myself. Maybe I'm really hurting from Kingsley and I'm just trying to keep it all squashed down inside my heart, not daring to let it all out.

Ugh.

Basically, things are just... *chaotic* at the moment, to say the least.

I storm through the front door of my flat into the kitchen to make myself a coffee. It's been another long day of handing out my CV to every place around. I'm literally looking for anyone that will take me now, but so far no one has. I'm starting to believe I'm the most un-hirable person on the freaking planet. Is it my face that's turning potential employers away? Do I just have a bad vibe around me?

Whatever it is, it is certainly not helping.

Three days of Kingsley not talking to me, and now I can't even find a job. My savings would all be dried up if it wasn't for that stupid thousand pounds Kingsley paid me for helping him with that self-tape.

Maybe I should start to think about heading home. Maybe this dream of living and working in this city is just too hard and always has been. Maybe I've been deluding myself since I've landed, and I don't actually belong here.

I take the coffee into the living room and fall, exhausted, on the sofa. I don't turn on the TV. I just lie there, warm cup between my hands, contemplating what a failure this whole London thing has been.

I was so close to making everything turn out right.

So freaking close.

My phone vibrates. It makes me jump in surprise and nearly makes me spill hot coffee all over myself.

Kingsley.

"Uh, hello?"

"Hi, Scarlett."

His familiar deep voice is so reassuring that I feel a shiver down my body. I feel warmth, and it isn't from the coffee.

"Kingsley. Wow. Long time, no hear."

"Yeah. Sorry I haven't been in touch. Things have been pretty crazy the last few days."

"What's gone on?" I ask him. "How are you?"

"Well, that's why I'm calling. I got the job."

"Wait, the self-tape job? The big Hollywood thing?"

"Yep."

I jump up from the sofa. "Wow. Congrats. That's amazing."

"Scarlett, I want to celebrate with you. After all, you did help me get it."

"Celebrate?"

"I'm taking you out for dinner."

"You don't have to do that, Kingsley. I just read some lines."

"No, I'm taking you out to celebrate. There's no refusal here. I need to do this after the week I've had. We're going out tonight."

"I've just got home," I reply nervously. "I'm super tired. I can't go out tonight."

Kingsley completely ignores my protests. "I'll be at yours in one hour. You better be ready for this date because I'm taking you, no matter how you're dressed. I'll sling you over my shoulder and flip you inside my car if I have to. You're coming with me."

I try to answer him. I try to refuse him.

242

But he hangs up.

I turn to the mirror and look at my reflection. I bite my lip. The man is impossible. He's making me fall for him. Hard. And with little choice in the matter. He's playing me like I'm a doll. If this continues any further, then I know my heart will be completely shattered when he eventually leaves me. To go out with him tonight is just going to hurt me in the future.

But I really, really want to see him.

I really, really want tonight.

Maybe I can use tonight to tell him I need a little bit of space. To back away a tiny bit to avoid my heart being totally crushed. Maybe I'll tell him about my thoughts of returning home to America and about our differences that Penelope highlighted the other day.

He did only introduce me to the director on the self-tape as his *friend*. Maybe I am only his friend. Maybe we should just remain friends.

I get changed. And even though my head is full of doubts, I let myself get excited for the date.

And then, as I check myself out again in the living room mirror, I hear a car horn honking outside.

Kingsley is here, right on the dot, and he wants me.

44

KINGSLEY

HOLY FUCK, *Scarlett looks like fire tonight.*

"You're beautiful," I tell her when she opens her flat door to me. The girl blushes shyly, adding more to how adorable she is.

"Shut up, Kingsley."

"I mean it. So damn *beautiful*."

She's wearing a stunning red dress that perfectly goes along with her hair. How can someone possibly look this good? My cock twitches in appreciation. I don't even want to go to dinner now, I just want to take her inside and fuck her senselessly.

Man, I've missed her, and it's only been three days. I mean, no other girl has made my heart ache like this. She's simply got a stranglehold over me, and I can't shake her loose. I don't even *want* to.

Scarlett follows me to my car, and I proceed to drive us into central London.

As she sits next to me, I can't help but let my eyes

secretly flicker over her fine body. I need to look at her again. It still makes me hard to think of the other morning when I strolled into my bedroom and took her for myself. To see how she looked at me as I fucked her into climax makes me feel so fucking tough. She completes me.

Scarlett sits in my car silent and still as we drive into town. Radiant. She truly is the most beautiful thing I have ever seen, but I want to prove that to her. I know she is cautious of me, and she has every right to be. Especially after America. I want her to know how now she's got me on my knees begging for her. One word from her and I'll plead right here and right now for her sweet pussy.

Sitting there, she doesn't know that she's actually tamed a wild Heath-Harding. There are certainly not many women in history to ever claim that. And the best thing is that it seems like Scarlett *doesn't even know* she has got me completely under her spell.

If only Duke could see me now with my heart pining after a girl...

The first thought I had today when my American agent called to say I've got the part in the big Hollywood movie was to tell Scarlett. She was the first person I thought of, and the only person I wanted to see. She's the only girl I can think of.

I take her to the Shard. It's the tallest building in Europe, a great tower that sits next to London Bridge station. It's mainly a fancy hotel, but tonight I'm taking Scarlett to one of the cool bars high up where you can see the whole of London through floor-to-ceiling glass windows.

She's floored by the view.

"I didn't know you could go to the top of this place," she says to me as we're shown to our seats by a waiter. "You're showing me the best sights of London."

"I knew you'd like it," I reply.

"I certainly do."

"Maybe you can repay me later," I whisper into her ear. "Maybe let's recreate that night in America when you took me in your mouth."

She blushes. "Not in public, Kingsley."

"I don't care what anyone else thinks. I want *you*, Scarlett. I want to feel your wet lips around my cock."

She giggles - embarrassed but also turned on – and slaps me playfully on the shoulder.

It's already night when we take our seats by the edge of the bar, right up against the window. The whole city circles us. I'm not an emotional man, but even I feel something when I look out on the view. Even I can tell this is super romantic.

"You like this?" I ask her.

"Oh, I love it."

I stare at her. She's a better sight than the view outside. She really is so stunning. Scarlett notices my gaze and turns her head towards the window, blushing again.

"Stop it," she mutters. "You're making me blush."

"I want to make you feel a lot of things, Scarlett," I reply. "Most of them too dirty to say out loud in a fancy bar."

"You're being so naughty, Kingsley."

"You're being even more naughtier wearing a dress like that," I reply in a low murmur. "I wish I could just tear it off you and have my way with you on this table right here with the whole of London watching from below."

"Well, you're just going to have to wait, aren't you? I'm not going to strip down just because you're horny. I'm here for a drink. Keep your dick in your pants for once."

I growl. She's a real tease.

And then I feel her heel under the table slowly make its

way up my leg. I growl again and bite my lip. Scarlett stares at me seductively.

Oh, she wants to feel power over me?

My hands grip around her smooth leg under the table. I've had enough of her teasing.

"Don't even tempt me, Scarlett," I whisper. "I'm *so very* close to forgetting all my social manners right now and ripping that tight little skirt off from around your pretty ass and giving you a spanking for the way you're playing with me. It's very naughty what you're doing."

"Maybe I do deserve to be punished," she replies.

I growl yet again. I must hold myself back from this woman.

And then our champagne arrives.

Saved by the bell.

"Cheers," I say to Scarlett as I pass her a glass.

"Cheers."

"Thank you for helping me get that acting job."

She blushes again. "I didn't *do* anything," she says.

"Yes, you did."

"I just read out some words, Kingsley. You were the one doing all the acting."

"Without you, I know I wouldn't be sitting here celebrating with you," I reply. Fuck, I really do mean it.

I've really gone soft, but that's what Scarlett has done to me. I can't help it.

"How are you with the whole murder thing?" she asks me.

I roll my eyes.

"It's not good," I reply.

"How's the case going?"

I sigh. "The police still have no idea who's done it. They've searched the theater a billion times, but still nothing. They don't even know the motive. I honestly don't know who would even want to kill Ben. It's just so fucking horrible."

"Wow. What are you going to do?"

"There's nothing I can do," I reply. "I mean, I've told the police I'm happy to help. I would actually like to visit the theater and have my own investigation of the stage. I might even hire some private investigators myself, but the police aren't budging on letting anyone into the Prestige Theater. It's impossible to look at the stage. In the meantime, I'm just going to keep my head down and work on this film."

"Sounds like a good plan," Scarlett says, nodding. She takes a sip of the champagne and - *fucking hell* - as if I don't want to launch across the table and kiss her square on her pretty mouth.

"What are you going to do?"

Scarlett shrugs. "I've been looking for a job all day."

"And?"

"Nothing."

"Shit."

"Yeah," she glances down at her napkin, playing with it nervously. "I'm thinking of maybe heading back to America."

Before I can respond to that shocking admission from the girl I adore, someone's finger suddenly points into my face.

"Ah, I knew I'd find you here."

Both Scarlett and I look up to see Penelope Jellis standing over us, dressed in a shiny dress that lights up the dim bar. Her blonde hair and makeup are immaculate as always, but her eyes are wide and pulsating with anger and astonishment.

"Penelope?" I ask the shaking woman. She's stormed up to our table like thunder. It's very overpowering. "What are you doing here?"

"Steve told me where you'll be tonight. He said you'll be celebrating here. Congratulations, *movie star*." Her voice is full of venom and spite. She doesn't look at Scarlett once.

I told Steve this evening about getting the job. He must've told Penelope. Damn.

"Thank you, Penelope," I reply, trying to diffuse the situation.

But that doesn't work.

"I really do need to congratulate you, King. You're going to be big, you know that? You're going to be a movie *star*."

Her voice raises higher and higher. Oh, I hear the sarcasm in her voice.

"Penelope, we're trying to have a quiet drink here," I reply.

It's then that she seems to notice Scarlett for the first time. Her head twists from the redhead back to me.

"You're having a *quiet drink* with *her*?"

"Yes, Penelope."

"A drink with a staff member from our theater?"

"Penelope..."

"You're an idiot, King. You haven't listened to me at all. What did I tell you the other week? What have all your friends told you? You're throwing away your family name for this American working minimum wage?"

I start to rise from my seat. She may mock me, but I am not going to let anyone mess with my girl. No one looks down on Scarlett when I'm around and gets away with it.

Scarlett's hand grabs mine before I lose control and launch a verbal attack on this actress.

"Leave it, Kingsley," she whispers. "She's right."

Her touch makes me freeze.

Penelope laughs, her eyes darting between us two.

"Of course I'm right. You've lost your mind, King. You're just playing with this poor girl's heart. You know

249

perfectly well you'll have to dump her before too long. What will your father think if you dared to bring this girl home? What will our friends think seeing you out and about with her?"

The whole bar has fallen silent, listening to this commotion. Penelope's theatrical voice can really carry across a room, especially when it's this loud.

Scarlett's eyes plead at me. She doesn't want to make a scene. I see her growing small at Penelope's words. I realize that she actually believes what Penelope is saying. I hate seeing her harmed like this. I hate seeing her lose that fiery spark I love so much.

It's too much for me.

I lean over to Penelope's ear. I whisper so that only she can hear.

"Fuck. Off. Bitch."

Her mouth drops in shock. I maintain my steel stare at her, my stare that goes straight into her soul. She's never heard - or seen - me like this.

But I am serious.

And she starts to see it.

With a dismissive scoff that's pitifully pathetic, she spins around and storms out of the bar, realizing she can't win. I would enjoy watching her walk away if I'm not so incredibly angry. She tries to hide her shame.

The entire bar is completely silent and motionless as I sit back down and take a sip of my champagne. I refuse to allow my night with Scarlett to be ruined by that crazy woman.

My redhead girl watches me.

"What did you just say to her?" she asks.

I don't want to talk about this.

"I told her what I really think of her."

Scarlett knows well enough not to probe further.

The bar resumes its noise, but Scarlett and I sit in quiet.

"She is right," Scarlett eventually quietly says. "We should not be together."

I lean across the table. "What are you saying?"

"I heard what she was saying to you in the dressing room before the murder," Scarlett says.

What?

My blood boils, but not at her. At Penelope. At her storming in and purposefully targeting my personal life like this. But Scarlett still continues. "Penelope is right. We are worlds apart. I mean, I am an American living above a fish and chip shop, and you are the son of a Lord, for goodness' sake. We shouldn't be sitting here together like this."

"No," I reply.

Scarlett blinks.

"What?"

"No. I reject all this. I reject that just because I'm a Heath-Harding that my future can be dictated by others. Not by Penelope. Not by my father. Not by history or family. I am my own man, and I am in love," I reply, finally letting it all out.

"What?"

"Fuck it, I'll say it. I'm in love with you, Scarlett."

She stares at me, gob smacked.

"You love me?" she asks, her voice trembling. Like she can't believe it.

She better believe it.

"I love you, Scarlett Hart. It's the goddamn truth."

She closes her eyes. Pauses. My heart races, waiting for her answer.

I swear, this woman knows how to keep me by the seat of my pants.

Then she opens her eyes, sighs, and finally speaks.

"I love you too, *King*."

"King?"

Scarlett eyes me up and down.

"Well, that's your name, isn't it?"

I nearly choke. "You're actually using my real name?"

She smirks. "Don't get used to it."

I lean back in my seat. I just heard my girl tell me she loves me and then use my nickname for the first time. I've completely forgotten all about Penelope Jellis.

I don't care what my friends think. I don't care what Father thinks. I don't care what the press or my family might think. Scarlett Hart just told me she loves me, and that's more than enough for me.

Love beats tradition. Love beats any obstacle.

Both Scarlett and I now know that love is the most powerful force in the world.

"No," I reply to my girl. "I want you to call me King for the rest of our lives, *Queen*."

45

KINGSLEY

"So, this is me," Scarlett says when we arrive back at hers. Sitting in the car, she looks up at her flat above the fish and chip shop whilst my eyes are completely focused on her body.

I wander over her creamy white thighs. Her supple breasts that teasingly poke through that thin dress of hers. Her plunging cleavage with those erect little nipples I want to grab and suck on. Her long slender legs that deliciously go on forever. And, of course, those soft plump lips I can worship all fucking day.

I am so hard right now for her, she wouldn't even believe.

I have been gagging to fuck her slowly since I saw her in her pretty dress at the door, but when she called me King at the Shard, then my body went full-on primal.

I want to fuck her with every fiber of my body. I *need* to fuck her.

I want to make sweet love to her.

I can feel the heat emanating from her from where I'm sitting. I have to remain still to rein my urges in. I still must act the honorable gentleman I was bred to be.

"This is you," I say.

Scarlett smiles at me and nods up to her flat. "You want to come in for a cup of tea upstairs?"

I chuckle. "I won't have one of your awful cups of tea," I reply. "But I will have a good American coffee."

Scarlett shakes her head and bites her lip. God, I love it when she does that. She must know how sexy she is when she acts all cute like that. She must know how she turns me on.

"Come on, then."

I turn off the ignition and eagerly follow her upstairs to her room. She hushes me to be quiet.

"My flatmate might be still asleep. We can't wake her."

Then we dive into her room. Scarlett doesn't even get the chance to turn the light on before I'm kissing her. Passionately. She falls back towards the wall, but I catch her in my arms. I pull her body towards me like she weighs nothing and continue to devour those pretty plump lips of hers. She has to raise herself to her tiptoes to reach my face, but I balance her in my hands.

Our kiss is a slow burn. The culmination of years of waiting for each other.

Scarlett puts up no resistance as I suddenly push her down onto her bed. The springs croak under the strength of my shove.

I am starving for her.

We tear the clothes off each other as we roll on her bed.

"You're like a beast," she admires as I rip off my underpants.

"You make me like this," I reply. "When I'm around you, I can't control myself."

I head straight for her inviting pussy that's glistening with her sweet juices. My hands greedily pull apart her legs and my tongue fucks her opening, making her gasp in such a sexy way.

I pant uncontrollably as my lips caress her vagina.

The effort I'm putting in seems to turn Scarlett on even more. Her hands ruffle my sweaty hair as she groans with every careful flick of my tongue over her throbbing clit.

It satisfyingly gets too much for her. She squeezes her thighs around my head as she pulls back from me and climaxes, her body shaking in total pleasure.

She rocks in waves.

It really makes me so fucking horny seeing how hard she is finished just because of my tongue.

"Oh, God," Scarlett repeats over and over. "Oh, God. Oh, God."

I lift my hand to her open mouth to hush her.

"Remember your flatmate."

Scarlett giggles.

"Screw her," she says as she opens her legs wide. "I don't care what noises I make when you can tease me like that. Fuck me, King."

I obey my fiery redhead girl.

I quickly sheath my big dick in a condom and lower myself into her. She's soaking wet for me as I slide in her hot pussy and start to fuck her nice and slow.

"Is this what you want?" I ask her.

"I can *feel* you, King," she replies, her eyes rolling to the back of her head. "God, I can really feel you inside me."

My hand whips around her waist and squeezes her juicy ass, and that's when I completely lose control. All tension flows out of me as I rock inside her, unable to hold back my inner urges anymore.

"You really need to be punished after that display at the Shard," I whisper threateningly in her ear.

She muffles something in reply, but I continue.

"You're my girl. You tried to control me in there. You tried to tease me with your sexy leg, but nobody teases me, you got that?"

My hand continues to cover her mouth. I feel her teeth nibbling at my fingers as I push her deeper into the bed with every thrust of my hips. She whimpers into my hand.

I'm like a firework ready to burst.

"I'm the one who gets to make you orgasm," I say. "I'm the one in control."

Her body squirms as I feel her cum again. That makes me go over the edge. We both moan together as I unload myself inside of her.

I hold her tight as I try to muddle my cries.

"You're so fucking strong, King," she whispers into my ear as I unload into her. "I want you. God, how I want you. You make me go wild."

Fuck me.

I collapse on top of Scarlett. Her arms wrap around me like she never wants to let me go. We lie there, panting. Basking in each other's glow.

Fuck, this girl makes me happy in ways I've never felt before.

Sweat trickles down my back as I lift myself to her ear.

"How about I fuck you again?" I whisper.

Scarlett moans in approval and my dick gets hard for another go.

46

SCARLETT

Kingsley - *King* - turns and pulls me in close to his big body, enveloping me in his warmth. His massive bicep curls around my breasts as he holds me like a precious trophy he doesn't want to let go of. I feel so safe in his arms. So secure.

He told me he loves me. That's all I've ever needed to hear from him. I know he's telling the truth. Plus, I saw it in his eyes last night as he made love to my body. Without a doubt, the man loves me.

As I lie here in his arms, I consider my future. America or Britain? Crystal River or London? I honestly don't know what the future might hold, but I know I am ready to face it with Kingsley by my side. It's us two versus the world.

One thing's for sure. There's a murder to solve. I will be with him, though, ready to face that challenge with my man. Ready to support him, no matter what.

But, as King had said, if someone was out to get his publicist, then they might be out for him. There are going to be dark and stressful days ahead, that's for certain.

But I don't want to think about all that now, not while I'm all tight and cozy against his firm body.

* * *

KING MAKES me his famous full English breakfast. He heaps it on the plate and hands it with a cheeky smile. He tries to grope my ass, but my hands swipe his away.

"This is enough to feed a small army," I say to him as he digs into his own plate across me on the table.

"I thought you'll be hungry after all that vigorous work last night." He winks at me. It's so infuriating, but really kind of sexy.

His incredible raspy morning voice fills me with heat. He leans down and nibbles my neck with his teeth. His lips suckle on my skin. A tingle flows through me and I swallow, ideas arising of ditching the cooking and taking him right back to my bed. My nipples harden as his three-day stubble on his perfect jawline brushes my collarbone. I sigh.

"Hello, you two."

Grace is standing at the door wearing her trademark dressing gown.

Oops. I forgot she's here.

"Hi, Grace," I say. "You've met King, right?"

She smiles at him goofily. "Yep, at the press party."

"Ah," Kingsley replies. "That was you who dragged Scarlett away from me."

"I don't let her talk to strange men. It's not a habit I encourage."

"No doubt. I appreciate that," Kingsley smirks. "Do you reckon I'm still a stranger?"

"I don't think you're too much of a stranger now," Grace says with a wink. "Scarlett's told me a *lot* about you."

"Oh, has she?"

"I've said nothing," I reply, blushing.

"Don't worry, King. It was nothing offensive. Quite the opposite."

"Shut up, Grace."

She cuddles me from behind. "You look very happy, Scarlett. A happy little morning glow. I bet you had a *very* restful night."

I growl at her. Kingsley smirks, his mouth full of food.

Grace doesn't care about embarrassing me. She's such a little shit-stirrer.

"Breakfast looks delicious," she says, squeezing my shoulders.

I point to my plate. "Help yourself. King here thought it'll be fine to raid our entire fridge."

Grace leans over my shoulder to scoop up a piece of bacon. "Thanks," she mumbles between greedy bites.

King's phone pings. He checks the message, and his face turns dark.

"What is it?" I ask him.

He looks at the phone seriously. Something is clearly very wrong.

"I don't believe it," he whispers.

"What, King?"

He looks up at me with a shocked expression. "It's from my brother."

"Your brother? What does he say?"

King takes his time to process what he's just read.

"It seems like someone has just made a threat against my life," he eventually says.

"What?" My jaw drops. Instantly, my beautiful morning shatters. My mind runs through all the possible scenarios. "Is it the same person who murdered Ben?"

He nods. "That's what my brother thinks. Someone's anonymously handed in a note to the police saying they're coming for me. The crazy thing is that the note has Ben's fingerprints all over it. Whoever's written this has his fingerprints and must certainly be involved in the murder. If they're not the murderer themselves."

"Jesus," Grace mutters.

"This changes everything," Kingsley says. He frowns. "I've got to go. I've got to sort this out right now."

I immediately stand. "Do you need me? I can come with you."

Kingsley shakes his head. "No. Please stay. The last thing I want is for you to get involved in this. I can't see you get hurt as well."

He bends over and kisses me delicately on the forehead.

"I've really got to go," he says. "I'll call you."

I can barely reply. I'm in shock. "Okay."

"I love you, Scarlett."

And then he's gone.

47

KINGSLEY

I CALL Duke the moment I get into my car. I've started the engine by the time he's picked up, so I switch the call over to loudspeaker as I speed through London's streets on the way home.

"Duke, what is it?"

My brother's deep voice resonates through the car.

"What we have so far is what I messaged you with," he says. "A letter was sent to the police, simply stating that they're coming for you. That's it. The thing has Ben's fingerprints all over it, so we know it's legit."

"It must be Ben's murderer, right?" I ask.

"It must be. I have no other explanation."

"Okay. This is serious, then."

"Are you okay, Kingsley? How are you feeling about all this?"

"I've got nothing on my mind except for *action*," I reply. "I want to get this sorted. And fast."

"Good man."

"Have you spoken to Father about this?"

"God, why would I? He'll only get involved and mess things up," Duke says. "He'll want to take control. No, we need to do this ourselves."

"Yep."

I quickly turn a corner. I think of Scarlett. Of last night. When she told me that she loves me. For her to get caught up in all of this mess would kill me.

She is the best thing that has ever happened to me, and I am not willing to lose that. I will *not* lose her. I will do everything in my power to protect the woman I love. I will not let some murdering asshole dare separate us.

It's like Duke can read my thoughts.

"And what about your girl, King? What will you do about her?"

"She is my top priority," I reply sternly. "I am going to make sure she is safe above everything else. I will lock her up in our family mansion to keep her away from this murderer if needs be."

Duke chuckles. "I'm sure she will put up a fight if you try to do that."

"I'm sure she will."

"I have yet to meet her, King. I very much would like to."

"You will soon," I say, and I mean it. My brother and the love of my life will have to meet, even if it's just to make me laugh to see them together in the same room. See that little fiery redhead up against my massive brother? It's a fight I don't know who'll win.

"That's a promise," Duke replies. "I very much would like to converse with the girl who's snared you. She must be quite the woman."

"Quite. You should meet her flatmate. I'm sure she'll give you a run for your money."

"I'm looking forward to it."

"Where are you now?" I ask.

"At our lawyer's office."

"We need to find this guy," I tell Duke. "We need to stop him."

"I am in full agreement," my brother replies.

"Good." I slam the brakes and spin the steering wheel, screeching my car into the opposite direction. I head down towards the center of London. "I am coming to pick you up, Duke. We're going to mine, and then we are sorting this shit out."

He hangs up. We're both on the same wavelength about this. We've got each other's back.

This has to end. Now.

I am a Heath-Harding, for goodness' sake. No asshole messes with us, or with our women. We'll sort this out.

But first I need to take care of my girl.

I pull over to the side of the road, take out my phone, and start to type a message to Scarlett.

48

SCARLETT

"THE MURDERER IS TARGETING *KING*?" Grace asks in disbelief the moment King walks out our front door.

I am in as equal disbelief as my flatmate.

Kingsley shrugged off the threat like it is nothing. Like it is something simple to work through. Like it is another script for him to memorize for an audition. He's all *action man* about it.

But it really isn't some game for him to work out. This is life and death, and this man – this killer *asshole* - is clearly out for Kingsley's blood.

I am so scared for my man. I want to be by his side for all of this, to make sure he is okay. To be there for him in his hour of need. I know he wants me with him, even if he can't bear to say it out loud.

"This is crazy," Grace says. "Why would someone go after him like this? Go after him acting like some comic book villain with all these threats? Do you know why?"

I shake my head.

"I guess they must be after him because of his family name," I reply, racking my brain for answers.

Grace stares at me blankly. I realize that when I introduced Kingsley to her, I did not mention his surname.

Right. She doesn't know who he is.

"Who?" she asks. "What family?"

"His family is some rich noble name that goes back so many generations," I reply. "Have you heard of them? Heath-Harding."

Grace reacts in a way I do not expect.

She gasps.

And then I realize that there's something deeper happening here. She definitely must've heard their name before. Something about King's last name is personal for Grace.

"I should've guessed," Grace whispers, her voice trembling. "I should've seen it the moment you introduced me to Kingsley. I should've put two and two together. He even *looks* like him, for goodness' sake."

"Who?" I ask, confused.

I don't get it.

"*Kingsley* Heath-Harding. Of course. It's such an unusual name. It should've rung alarm bells from the moment I saw him."

It's like she's talking to herself more than she's talking to me. Like she's reminding herself of something.

"What are you saying, Grace? I don't understand you."

Her gaze matches mine. Shock and horror and a twinkle of happy recognition all flash across her face at once.

"I know his brother. Duke Heath-Harding."

Now I'm the one who's flabbergasted.

"What? You know Duke? You're friends?"

I haven't even met King's brother, and now Grace is saying she knew him?

"I know him more than just *friends*," Grace replies, smiling. "We had a thing. Years ago."

"A thing?"

"We kinda dated," Grace says. She scoffs, still in total disbelief at the situation. "A long time ago. He's the boy who got away. The boy who broke my heart."

"Wow. Everything is happening at once," I say, sitting back down in the chair. I need something to support my weight. All this. The murder. King telling me he loves me. And now Grace saying she had a *thing* with his brother? It's all too much to handle in one morning. "You need to tell me every single detail."

"And you're in love with Kingsley Heath-Harding? He was in my flat? No *freaking* way," Grace mutters. "I wonder what Duke will do when he realizes all this. When he realizes who I am."

I'm about to ask her all about it - to tell me everything - when my phone pings with a message. I check it.

It's Kingsley.

My heart stops as I quickly unlock my phone and read what he's sent me.

WHATEVER'S GOING ON, *Scarlett, I just want you to know that I love you. I've loved you from the moment I saw you carrying that stupid Shakespeare book outside Crystal River High. I've loved you when you refused to call me King. I've loved you when you licked that dollop of clotted cream off that scone at the London Grand Hotel in that super sexy way. I've loved you when you helped me do that audition, even though I could see you were petrified of acting again. I loved you when you sat across from me in the bar at the Shard and told me you loved me. I will make the world safe for you, I promise. I need you to stay home and stay safe. I need you to wait for me to tell you everything's okay. Will you do that for me, Scarlett?*

"Grace," I say, looking up at my flatmate from my phone. "You have to tell me the full story between you and Duke. You really have to. But right now, I have to sort something out."

She nods. "Okay."

"I need to leave," I say.

"Right."

I glance back at King's message. At his final lines telling me to stay home like I'm some kind of captive housewife. He's going to make everything safe for me while I just dutifully sit at home like I'm some precious trophy of his?

"Not on my watch," I say before I pocket the phone and head out the front door.

49

SCARLETT

I'm not letting no man hide me away.

Not even if it's the man I love.

I storm right out of the flat and wave down a passing black cab.

"Where to?" the Cockney taxi driver asks me, turning around in his seat.

I know exactly where I'm going.

I am going to Kingsley's.

He wants me to sit at home on my ass and not do a damn thing? Well, not if I have something to say about it, even if there is a murderer on the prowl.

When I arrive, I bang on the door to Kingsley's penthouse apartment. The loud noise of my knocking echoes down the hallway, which, eventually, Kingsley opens up.

I sense his shock and uneasiness at my sudden presence at his door.

"Scarlett?" he asks, his voice high. "What are you doing here?"

I press my finger into his chest and don't let him get another word in.

"You may be incredibly rich and incredibly famous and incredibly good-looking," I say to Kingsley as he stares, wide-eyed, at me. "But I want to make one thing clear. We're going to be equals. No matter if there's a murderer out to get you or not. If you can't accept that we are equals in this together, then you can't have me. You got it? I hope you're man enough for me."

A man pokes his head out from behind Kingsley. He looks just like him, but maybe a tiny bit taller. And he's clean-shaven. And a few years older.

Clearly his brother.

There's a long pause after my little spiel. No one speaks. And then King's brother smirks.

"She's got you there, King," the guy says. "What do you say?"

Kingsley rolls his eyes at him.

"You must be Duke," I say, offering out a hand.

"Yes, I am," Duke Heath-Harding says. "And you must be Scarlett. You're as pretty as King says you are."

He shakes my hand and smiles.

"It's pretty intimidating being in the presence of two Heath-Harding boys," I remark. Kingsley doesn't laugh, but his brother does.

"Can I have a moment of privacy?" King asks his brother.

"Well, this seems serious," Duke says. "I'll leave you two alone."

He squeezes past us into the hallway and heads for the elevator.

"It was good to meet you, Duke."

He winks at me as the elevator doors ding open. "I'm sure I'll be seeing a lot more of you around, Scarlett. King,

I'll message you. We'll sort out this investigation once you've spoken to your girl, alright?"

King nods and Duke disappears into the elevator.

"So," I say, turning back to King. "You understand what I'm saying?"

"I understand, Scarlett. You've made it very explicit."

"So, are you man enough for me?"

"Oh, I've got you loud and clear, Scarlett," Kingsley says seriously. "I can handle you. I'm man enough for whatever you throw at me."

"I am in control of my destiny, Kingsley," I reply sternly. "You can't just keep me hidden away, okay? I'm not some princess needing to be kept in an ivory tower."

He smiles in that super sexy way of his and shakes his head at me. "You want to talk about control, Scarlett? You've had control over me ever since that sunny day I first saw you," he says. "You've always been the one in control over my heart."

His words penetrate my soul. His grip on me is total. This man has my love.

"I know what Penelope says, and it is true," I tell him, wanting to get everything out. I want to lay out all my thoughts on the table before we launch into anything else. I want him to know all my hopes and dreams and fears. I want him to know what I've been dreading about for the last few weeks. "We *are* worlds apart, but I am willing to be with you. I am willing to work on us, no matter how hard that might be. And it will be hard, there's no doubt about that. Do you feel the same?"

"Fuck tradition," King replies coldly. "Fuck what others think. We love each other, and love trumps everything."

That's it. The words I want to hear. He's willing to do anything for us, even go above his own family name.

He truly loves me.

And then he pulls me close. He kisses me deeply, and then he whispers into my ear.

"Now I want you to get into my bed."

50

KINGSLEY

Scarlett Hart is more than just some ordinary girl.

If I didn't know that already, then I certainly know it now. She's come storming to my penthouse with that trademark fiery spark of hers to demand that I be a man and accept her for who she is. To demand me to not keep her as some treasure. To demand that we are partners.

She's really got some backbone; I'll give her that.

But she has absolutely no need to demand anything. Her lips are soft when I kiss them in my front doorway.

She wanted me to prove myself to her. She didn't want me to be a guy that will just dump her in the gutter.

Well, I'm not that kind of guy.

I will give this girl the whole fucking world if only she just asked me.

Next to her, my name means nothing. My money means nothing. My fame means nothing. My family means nothing.

Scarlett Hart means everything to me.

And I want her to know that.

And I'm going to prove that to her right now.

51

SCARLETT

KING TAKES me with a force I've never even experienced from him. It's like he's showing off. And I'm certainly not complaining.

He pulls me into his penthouse and into his bed. I willingly fall into his strong arms as he practically carries me into his bedroom. He flings me down on the bed so that I'm lying face-up and kisses me forcefully. Our tongues play as his fingers dance along my body. He fondles my tits, and I shiver at his touch.

"I'm going to *savor* you," he whispers into my ear. I can hear my heart beating as he hungrily pulls me out of my shorts. "Savor you nice and slow."

I moan as his lips part mine again and he slowly makes his way down the length of my body. His hands prise open my legs and soon enough I feel my panties being lowered. His warm fingers find my pussy and I gasp.

"Oh, King."

"You're so wet for me," he says. "You're always so wet for me. I like it."

"I'm always wanting you," I reply, breathless. "I can never stop thinking about you."

"And that's how I know you're all mine."

His tongue brushes the edge of my clit and I go wild. I squirm, trying to hold back a squeal of pleasure. I'm unsuccessful. Very much unsuccessful.

My head is full of King. His intense glare at me. The way he smiles at me. The sheer freaking confidence of the man. I can't believe he's mine. All mine.

"I love your taste," he says before he wraps his mouth around my eager pussy and makes my world rock. My legs press against his face, as I can no longer control myself. I have to stop myself from wriggling about on the bed in involuntary pleasure as his tongue plays with my clit.

Heat surges through me.

I'm brought to the very precipice of orgasm.

"That's it, that's it," I scream as waves of delight flow through my body. "King, I'm all yours. *I'm all yours.*"

My God, it's so freaking hot.

Panting, I close my eyes and lean back into his soft bed as I continue to feel swells of bliss ripple through me.

King rises above me. His erect cock glistens in the dim bedroom light. His hard muscles look so imposing.

"My turn," he says with a ravenous gleam in his eyes.

I have no objections to what he wants to do to me.

And what he does do to me is to proceed to fuck me into oblivion.

* * *

KING and I lie in his bed. Content and completely spent. We both drift in and out of a euphoric sleep, perfectly fulfilled.

If this is what life is going to be with this man, then give it to me every damn day.

"You alright?" he asks me in a mellow voice, barely raising his head off the pillow. His eyes lazily open and close.

I beam at him.

"I'm more than alright."

"Good, because when I've had a nap, I am coming back for round two."

I kiss his soft lips. "I'm ready for you," I reply.

And then he slides off into a deep sleep.

I know that everything was against us being together. We're from two different countries, separated by time and distance. Small town America meets rich aristocratic London.

Really, two completely different worlds. We shouldn't even have had a chance at meeting, let alone falling in love.

But fate has brought us together. We met once, and now we've had a second chance at love.

And I am prepared to take that opportunity with both hands. I am prepared to love this gorgeous sexy hunk of a man forever, no matter what asshole murderer tries to get in the way.

He is my King, and I am his Queen.

EPILOGUE

SCARLETT

Even though Kingsley wants me to stay safe, there is absolutely no way I'm going to sit back like a good little girl and let all this happen to him. I know he says he and Duke are formulating plans to get this murderer, but damn it if I'm not allowed to play my own part.

And I've got something I can do that might help.

Something that Duke and King, even with all their money and connections and manly power, can't do.

I know how to sneak into the Prestige Theater.

I can do my own little investigation of the stage.

I break into the theater using the very same side exit I was so crap at guarding when I was working as an usher. The one Giles told me off about for accidentally letting customers through during the shows.

I sneak in through there and onto the stage. I'm all on my own. No one else knows what I'm doing, not even King. I know I really shouldn't be here, but I need to help with this investigation. I need to do something.

I start to look around the stage. Clearly, no one has been here since the crime except for forensics and the police. There's blue police tape everywhere. It's all very dusty. I use my phone's torch to scan around for any clues the police might've missed. I take some photos to show King and Duke. I scour around like I'm Nancy freaking Drew.

You know what? I'm pretty good at this. After all, I have watched hundreds of hours of true crime documentaries with Grace.

There's an eerie silence within the theater. This place should not be quiet, it should really be full of noise. Of speeches. Of music. Of applause. It's now just so dark and cold and lifeless.

I tiptoe around, not wanting to disturb anything. I take some more photos of the stage.

I stand right in the middle of it so that I can look out over the seats in the auditorium. This was where King acted every night, where a lot of actors have been performing for over a hundred years. There must be a lot of ghosts in this place. A lot of memories. Stolen kisses. Gossip. Criminal activities.

And now a murder.

I can't stop thinking that this was where Ben was found. What a horrible way to die, having your throat slit in the dark.

And the killer is still on the loose...

The thought sends a shiver down my spine.

I take a moment to breathe. It's very scary being in here; maybe I should head on out. I don't want to be in here any longer than necessary. I don't like it here in the darkness.

And then, in the silence, I hear something behind me. A scraping on the floor.

At first, I think it's a rat.

But it's too loud for a pest.

It's human footsteps.

Coming straight at me in the dark. Getting faster and faster.

I turn, knowing there's nowhere for me to run. I'm standing right in the middle of the stage.

A figure emerges from the darkness, heading towards me.

A person.

And I scream.

WANT to read what happens next?

Go to rebeccacastle.com to find the links for Duke (London Boys #2)

ABOUT THE AUTHOR

Rebecca has had the storytelling bug since... forever!

What Rebecca likes most is writing steamy hot filthy romances with sweet happy endings sprinkled with some delicious bad boys.

Born and raised in an Aussie coastal town, she loves travelling around the world - meeting new people and discovering their stories.

Aside from adventuring she also enjoys a good rainy day in with a good book or at a hot beach catching the sun.

She's a world-class napping professional. You'll most likely find her asleep snuggled up on a sofa somewhere cozy.

For other titles and information please visit
rebeccacastle.com

facebook.com/rebeccacastleauthor
instagram.com/rebeccacastle.author

Made in the USA
Monee, IL
30 May 2023

34947857R00173